The man was short and stocky, with a beefy red face and hard eyes. 'Have your fun,' he said, 'while you're able. You won't last long. These folks don't take kindly to no brash stranger comin' in here tryin' to run a blazer on 'em. Joe Neal was hung. He got his neck stretched nigh two weeks ago. You go on out to the ranch, but you better have a gun in your hand. Lud Fuller's fast.'

'Is he?' Blaine chuckled. 'I've known a few fast men.'

'You watch your step, Utah. Not even you could stop this bunch if they get started. Every man in this country has been poised and ready to jump at the 46 range. They've wanted it too long, and this is the first excuse they've had. It would take a hard, gun-fightin' outfit to hold it now, one man could never do it.'

'Any of that crowd that could be trusted?'

'I doubt it. When you ride on to 46 range, you ride alone . . . '

Also by Louis L'Amour

UTAH BLAINE

Louis L'Amour

A STAR BOOK
published by
the Paperback Division of
W. H. ALLEN & Co. PLC

A Star Book
First published in Great Britain by Universal-Tandem
Publishing Co. Ltd, 1972
Reprinted June 1974
Reprinted May 1975
Reprinted in 1976, 1979, 1982, 1985 by
the Paperback Division of W. H. Allen & Co. PLC
44 Hill Street, London W1X 8LB

Originally published in the United States under the pen-name
'Jim Mayo' by Ace Books, Inc., 1954
Copyright © 1954 by Ace Books, Inc. All rights reserved

Printed and bound in Great Britain by
Anchor Brendon Ltd, Tiptree, Essex

ISBN 0 352 30824 X

CHAPTER I

HE WAS ASLEEP and then he was awake. His eyes flared wide and he held himself still, staring into the darkness, his ears reaching for sound.

He could smell the dry grass on which his blankets were spread and he could smell the night. And then he heard again the sound that had awakened him. It was the stir of hoofs on the dusty trail some thirty yards away—not the sound of one horse alone, but of several horses.

Carefully, he lifted himself to one elbow. This was strange country and he was unarmed. What motives might inspire whoever was out there he could not guess, but large groups of riders do not move silently along midnight trails without adequate reason.

This was no celebrating bunch of cowhands headed for the home ranch. These men were quiet, and their very stillness was a warning. No stranger to trouble, he lay perfectly still, feeling the muscles back of his ears tighten with suspense.

They had stopped. A horse moved nervously, and then there was a voice. "Right above your head." There was a pause. "That's it."

Another and deeper voice spoke. "Lead his horse over here." There was movement, a click of hoof on stone. "Hold it."

Saddle leather creaked, easily heard in the still night air. Then that second voice came again. "There!"

The word held satisfaction, a gloating born from some dark well of hatred and rolled on the tongue as if the speaker had waited long for this moment and wished to prolong it.

"Easy with that horse!" There was harsh impatience. "Don't let him drop! Ease him down! I want him to know what he's gettin'!"

"Hurry it up!" The voice held impatience and obvious distaste. "Do it, if you're goin' to, an' let's get out of here!"

"Take it easy!" There was a snarl in the deep voice. "I'm runnin' this show an' I've waited too long for this chance. How d'you like it, Neal?"

The voice that spoke now was that of the man being hanged. He spoke coldly. "You always were a doublecrossin' rat, Lud, an' you ain't changed any."

There was the sharp crack of a slap, and then the same voice spoke again. "Lucky my hands are tied, Lud. Old as I am I'd take you apart."

There was another blow, and the sharp creaking of leather that implied more blows. The man in the blankets was sweating. He eased from the blankets and grasped his boots, drawing them on. Then he stood up.

"Hurry it up, Lud! It'll soon be light an' we've miles to go!"

The listener held himself still. To be found here would mean certain death, and he was utterly defenseless. Against one man, or even two, he might have taken a chance, but without a gun he was helpless against this number.

This was no committee of honest citizens but some dark and ugly bunch out to do business that demanded night and secrecy. They could not afford to be seen or known.

"All right," Lud's voice was thick, irritated, "lead his horse out easy. I want this to last."

A horse moved and the listener heard the creak of a rope taking strain; then he heard the jerking of it as the hanged man kicked and struggled. The listener knew. He had seen a lynching before this.

"Never thought I'd live to see the day," the first speaker said. "After Neal the rest of them will be easy. This was the one had me bothered."

"Huh!" Lud grunted. "You leave it to me. This was the one I wanted. Now we'll get the rest. Let's get out of here!"

There was a sudden pound of horses' hoofs and the listener moved swiftly. Yet it was a movement without sound. Like a shadow he slid into the brush, the branches not even whispering on his clothing.

The chance was slight, but there was a chance. The last few feet he ran soundlessly on the thick leaves and grass. He went up the tree with swift agility and with a quick slash, he cut the rope and let the body tumble into the dust. Grasping the branch he swung out and dropped lightly beside the body, then bent swiftly and loosened the noose. Almost at once the man began to gasp hoarsely.

So far as could be seen the trail was empty, but this was no healthy place. Picking up the older man as if he were a child, the rescuer went quickly through the brush to his bed and placed the man on the ground. Then he loosened the man's shirt and got his own canteen. Gasping painfully, his neck raw from the manila rope, the man drank. Then he sank back on the blankets.

Restlessly, the young man paced, staring up the

trail through the brush. One of the riders might come back, and the sooner they got away from here, the better. He knew the folly of mixing in other people's business in a strange country.

The old man lay on the ground and stared up at the sky. His fingers fumbled at the raw flesh of his throat and came away bloody. His gray eyes turned toward his rescuer. "Fig . . . figured they . . . had me." his voice was thick and hoarse.

"Save the talk. Only reason you're alive is that Lud hombre. He wanted you to choke slow instead of break your neck with a drop."

The old man rolled over to his elbow and sat up. He stared around, looking at the two worn blankets, then at the canteen. He took it in trembling hands and drank slowly. Then he said, "Where's your horse?"

"Don't have one."

The older man stared at him. The young man's possessions appeared to be nothing but the blankets and canteen. The flannel shirt he wore was ragged and sunfaded, the jeans did not fit him, and he had no hat. His only weapon was a Bowie knife with a bone handle. Yet beneath the ragged shirt the shoulders and chest bulged with raw power and the man's face was hard and brown, his green eyes steady. Moreover there was about him a certain undefined air of command that arrested the older man's curiosity.

"My name's Joe Neal," he volunteered. "Who are you? What are you?"

The big man squatted. He reached for a piece of brown grass and snapped it off. "What's this all about?" he jerked his head at the trail. "Who were they?"

"Vigilantes," Neal's voice was still hoarse. "That's the devil of it, stranger. I helped organize 'em."

He stretched his neck gingerly. His face was brown and seamed with wrinkles. "My brand's the 46 Connected. The country was overrun with rustlers so we got them vigilantes together. Them rustlers was well organized with spies everywhere. Nobody ever knew who was behind 'em until Lud Fuller turned it up that Gid Blake was the man. I'd never have believed it."

"They hung him?"

"Nope. He got him a gun first an' shot it out. Fuller handled it."

"Blake a gambler?"

"Lord, no! He was a rancher. The B-Bar, almost as big as my outfit."

The man got to his feet. "If you're up to it, we better light out. Is there anywhere near we can pick up horses?"

"The nearest is over by the lava beds. The Sostenes' outfit."

"Sostenes? A Mex family?"

"Uh huh. Been here a long time."

They started walking, heading back up a draw. When they reached a ledge of rock the stranger stepped over to it. "Better keep to this. They'll trail us. Sounded like they wanted you mighty bad."

Neal's muscles were still jumping nervously from the shock of hanging. Sweat got into the raw flesh on his throat and smarted painfully.

He scowled as he walked, feeling with his brain for the answer to the problem that confronted him. Why had they done this to him? He had never dreamed that Lud might hate him, although he had always secretly despised the big man. The vigilante notice had come to him shortly before mid-

9

night and he had answered it all the more promptly because he felt it was time to disband. He was not at all satisfied about the hanging of Gid Blake and he knew the community had been profoundly shocked. He had joined the riders at their rendezvous and had been promptly struck over the head from behind. By the time he shook himself out of it, he was tied and they were taking him to the tree.

He turned and glanced at the big man who walked behind him with an effortless ease that he could never have hoped to match. Not even, he reflected, as a young man.

Who was the fellow? What was a white man doing with no more outfit than a digger Indian?

After awhile, Neal stopped. "Better take a blow." He grinned wryly. "Never was no hand for foot travel, not even when I felt good. And it's a distance yet."

"Got any plans?"

"No," Neal admitted, "I haven't. This thing has been a shock to me. Can't figure why they did it. One of the men in that oufit was my foreman. Now I don't know who to trust."

"Then don't trust anybody."

"That's easier said than done. I've got to have help."

"Why?" The big man leaned back on the ground. "Folks who want to help mostly just get in the way. This here's a one-man job you got."

Neal felt gingerly of his neck. "I'm not as young as I used to be. I don't want to go back there an' get my neck stretched."

"You aim to quit?"

Neal spat. "Like hell, I'll quit! Everything I've got

is back there. You want I should give up thirty thousand head of cattle?"

"Be a fool if you did. I figured you might send me."

"You?"

"Sure. Give me papers authorizing me as ranch manager, papers the banks will recognize. Let me work it out. You're up against a steal, and a smart one."

"I don't follow you."

"Look, you organized the vigilantes to get rid of some crooks. Then all of a sudden when you aren't with them the vigilantes hang this Gid Blake. He was a big rancher, you said. What happens to his outfit?"

"What happens? His daughter runs it."

"Can she?"

"Well, I don't know," Neal admitted. "She's mighty young."

"Was her foreman a vigilante? I'm bettin' he was. I'm bettin' somebody got smart down there and decided to use the vigilantes to get possession of your range and that of Blake. From what they said they have others in mind, too. I'm bettin' none of your range was filed on. I'm bettin' that with you gone they just move in. Is that right?"

"Could be." Neal shook his head. "Man, you've struck it. I'll bet that's just it." He shook his head. "I can't figure who would boss a deal like that."

"Maybe nobody. Maybe just two or three put their heads together and got busy. Maybe when the job is done they'll fight among themselves."

"Who would stop it? Is there anybody down there who might try?"

"Tris Stevens might. Tris was marshal once, years ago, and he's still right salty. Ben Otten might, he's smart enough. Blake, Otten, Nevers and me, we were the big outfits. Lee Fox was strong but not too big. It was us decided on the vigilantes, although I was the ringleader, I expect."

They got up and started on, walking more slowly. "Well, like my proposition? You go back there now they'll kill you sure as shootin'. Send me in an you'll have 'em worried. They won't know what's become of you, whether you're dead or alive."

"I'd have to be alive to send you down there."

"No, not if you pre-dated the order, say two months or even a couple of weeks. Then I could move in and they would be some worried."

"What's to stop 'em from killin' you?" Neal demanded. "You'd be walkin' right into a trap."

"It wouldn't be the first. I'll make out."

They walked on and the sun came out and it grew hotter, much hotter. Joe Neal turned the idea over in his mind. He was no longer a youngster. Well past sixty, with care he might live for years. But he wasn't up to fighting a lone hand battle. While this fellow—he liked his looks.

"I don't know who you are. Far's I can see you're just a tramp without a saddle."

"That's what I am. I just broke jail."

Neal chuckled. "You got a nerve, stranger. Tellin' me that when you're askin' me to drop my ranch in your lap."

"The jail was in Old Mexico. I was a colonel in the army of the revolution, and the revolution failed. They took me a prisoner and were fixin' to shoot me. The idea didn't appeal very much so I went through the wall one night and headed for Hermosillo, then made it overland to here."

"What's your name? I s'pose you got one?"

The young man paused and mopped the sweat from his face. "I got one. I'm Utah Blaine."

Joe Neal stiffened, looking up with startled realization. "You . . . you're Utah Blaine? *The gunfighter?*"

"That's right."

Joe Neal considered this in silence. How many stories had he heard of Blaine? The man was ranked for gun skill with Wes Hardin, Clay Allison and Earp. He had, they said, killed twenty men. Yet he was known as a top hand on any ranch.

"You took a herd up the trail for Slaughter, didn't you?"

"Yeah. And I took one up for Pierce."

"All right, Blaine. We'll make a deal. What do you want?"

"A hundred a month and an outfit. A thousand dollars expense money to go in there with. I'll render an account of that. Then if I clear this up, give me five hundred head of young stuff."

Neal spat. "Blaine, you clear this up for me and you can have a thousand! A permanent job, if you want it. I know how to use a good man, Blaine, and if you were good enough for old Shanghai Pierce you are good enough for me. I'll sign the papers, Blaine, makin' you ranch manager and givin' you right to draw on my funds for payrolls or whatever."

They came up to the Sostenes ranch at sundown. For a half hour they lay watching it. There were three men about: tall old Pete Sostenes and his two lanky sons. It was a lonely place to which few people came. Finally, they went down to the ranch.

Pete saw them coming almost at once and stood waiting for them. He glanced from Blaine to Neal. "What has happen'?" he asked. "You are without horses! You have been hurt."

Inside the house, Neal explained briefly, then nodded to Blaine. "He's goin' back there for me. Can you get us out of here to the railroad? In a covered wagon?"

"But surely, *Señor!* An' if I can help, you have only to ask."

Four days later, in El Paso, they drew up the papers and signed them. Then the two shook hands. "If I had a son, Utah, he might do this for me."

"I reckon he would," Blaine replied, "an' I've got a stake in this now, Neal. You want your outfit back, and I want to start a little spread of my own."

The dust from the roadbed settled on his clothes. Come hell or high water, Blaine thought. But he knew it was foolish to make promises. It was action that mattered, and now he was ready for action. He liked the feel of the gun in his waistband, and the knowledge of the other guns in his bag and the cased Winchester beside him.

Red Creek was the name of the town. First he had to hit Red Creek, then head for the 46 Connected. Utah Blaine slumped in the train seat and pulled his new hat over his eyes. He had better rest while he had the chance.

CHAPTER II

UTAH BLAINE reached Red Creek at high noon and helped unload his horse from the baggage car. Persuasion supplemented by ten dollars had assured the passage of the stallion.

It was a line back dun with a black face, mane and tail. Short coupled and powerful, the horse showed his Morgan ancestry in conformation but there was more than a hint of appaloosa or other Indian stock in his coloring, and in a few other characteristics. From the moment Utah glimpsed the stallion he had eyes for no other horse.

When he had the horse off the train he saddled up with his new saddle and bridle, then slipped his Winchester into the scabbard and mounted. He walked the horse up the street to the livery stable, aware that both he and the stallion were being subjected to careful examination.

It was a one-street town with hitching rails before most of the buildings. The bank was conveniently across from the livery stable. Beyond the stable was the blacksmith shop, facing a general store across the street. There was a scattering of other buildings and behind them, rows of residences, some of the yards fenced, most of them bare and untended.

Blaine stabled his horse and came to the door of the building to smoke. Two men sat on a bench at the door of the stable facing the water trough. They were talking idly and neither glanced his way although he knew they were conscious of his presence.

". . . be fighting for months," one of them was saying, "an' we all know it. Nobody around here could buck Lud Fuller, an' I don't reckon anybody will try."

"I ain't so sure about that," the other man objected. "The 46 Connected is the best range around here. Better than the B-Bar or any of them. I wouldn't mind gettin' a chunk of it myself."

Utah Blaine stood there in the doorway, a tall, broad-in-the-shoulder man with narrow hips and a dark face, strong but brooding. He wore a black flat-brimmed flat-crowned hat and a gray wool shirt under a black coat. His only gun was shoved into his waistband.

He stepped to the door and glanced briefly at the men. "If you hear talk about the 46 bein' open range," he said briefly, "don't put any faith in it. Joe Neal isn't goin' to drop an acre of it."

Without waiting to see the effect of his remarks he started diagonally across the street toward the bank. Even the dust under his feet was hot. Up the street a hen cackled and a buckboard rounded a building and came down the street at a spanking trot. A girl was driving and she handled the horses beautifully.

Blaine threw his cigarette into the dust. Stepping into the coolness of the bank building, he walked across toward a stocky built man with sandy hair who sat behind a fence at one side of the room. On the desk there was a small sign that read: Ben Otten.

"Mr. Otten? I'm Blaine, manager of the 46 Connected. Here's my papers."

Otten jerked as if slapped. "You're what?"

His voice was so sharp that it turned the head of the teller and the two customers.

Blaine placed the packet of papers before Otten. "Those will tell you. Mr. Neal is taking a vacation. I'm taking over the ranch."

Ben Otten stared up into the cool green eyes. He was knocked completely off balance. For days now little had been talked about other than the strange disappearance of Joe Neal and its probable effect on Red Creek. There wasn't a man around who didn't look at the rich miles of range with acquisitive eyes. Ben Otten was not the least of these. Neal, it had been decided, was dead.

No body had been found, but somehow word

had gotten around that the vigilantes had accounted for him as they had for Gid Blake. Not that it was discussed in public, for nobody knew who the vigilantes were and it was not considered healthy to make comments of any kind about their activities.

At first, two gamblers had been taken out and lynched. Others had been invited to leave town. That, it was generally agreed, had been a good thing—a move needed for a long time. However, the attempted lynching and eventual killing of Gid Blake had created a shock that shook the ranching community to its very roots. Still, Blake *might* have been involved in the rustling. Then Joe Neal vanished, and the one man who had questioned the right of his disappearance had been mysteriously shot.

Another man, a loyal Neal cowhand, had likewise been killed. Nobody mentioned the reasons for these later killings but the idea got around. It was not a wise thing to talk in adverse terms of the vigilantes.

Despite this, Ben Otten had been giving a lot of thought to the vast 46 range and the thirty thousand head of cattle it carried. After all, somebody was going to get it.

Otten was aware that Lud Fuller imagined himself to be first in line, and Nevers, while saying little, was squaring around for trouble. Information had come to Otten that Nevers had quietly eased several hundred head of his cattle to 46 range and that his line cabins nearest to the 46 were occupied by several men to each cabin. Nobody was going to get that range without a fight. And now this stranger had come.

Opening the manila envelope Otten took out the papers and examined them. There was a letter addressed to him, advising that Michael J. Blaine had been appointed manager of the 46 holdings with full authority to sign checks, to purchase feed if necessary, or any and all things appertaining to the successful management of the ranch.

There was a power of attorney and several other papers that left no doubt of Blaine's position. Otten knew the signature well, and there could be no doubt of it. Joe Neal was alive. Moreover, he scowled, these papers were dated some weeks prior to this day.

Otten looked up. "These seem to be in order, but I'm afraid I don't understand. Where is Joe?"

"I left him in El Paso, but he's not there now. In fact, he told me he wanted a vacation. I doubt if he'll be back here for several months, or even a year."

Otten leaned back, chewing on his cigar. "Have you got any idea what you're steppin' into?"

"More or less."

"Well, let me say this. You'll have few friends. Neal was a well-liked man, but there was envy around. When he disappeared nearly everybody began maneuvering to get a piece of his spread. Some of them have been counting on it pretty strong, and you'll have trouble."

"I'm no stranger to it," Blaine said quietly, "but I'm not huntin' it."

He picked up a letter from among the papers. This informed all and sundry that Blaine was manager of the ranch with complete authority to hire, fire or purchase. It was signed by Neal and two witnesses, both of them known locally as prominent El Paso businessmen.

"Get the word around, will you?" Blaine suggested. "I'm going out to the ranch in the morning. I hope there'll be no trouble."

"There will be."

Blaine turned toward the door and then stopped. The girl who had driven the buckboard was coming through the door, walking swiftly. As she walked she peeled the gloves from her hands. She was about five feet and four inches and very pretty. Her eyes were deep blue, her hair red gold. She was apparently angry.

"Ben, have you heard anything from the capitol? Are they sending a man up here to investigate my father's murder?"

"Now, Mary, you know they can't be sendin' men all over the state to look into ever' little squabble. We're all sorry about Gid, but it just ain't no use to fret."

"Another thing. I want you to find me a new foreman. Miller is getting completely out of hand. He's even claiming the range now. Says I'm a woman and can't hold range."

Otten got up. His face was square and brown. He looked more the successful cattleman, which he was, than the banker. He was worried now, but obviously uncertain as to what course to adopt. "There's no law says a woman can't hold range, Mary, you know that. But I reckon it won't be easy. You'll have to fight for it just like Blaine, here."

She turned sharply and seemed to see Utah for the first time. "Blaine? I don't know the name. What are you fighting for?"

"He's manager for Joe Neal, Mary. Come from El Paso to take over."

"Manager for Joe Neal?" She was incredulous. "I don't believe it! What would Joe want a manager for? Anyway, Joe Neal's dead, and you know it as well as I do. If this man says he's Neal's manager, he's lying."

19

Utah smiled from under his eyebrows. "Those are hard words, Ma'am. An' Joe Neal is alive—and well."

"He couldn't be!"

"Sorry, Ma'am, but he is."

"But I was told—!" she broke off sharply. Then she said, "We heard the vigilantes got him."

"He's alive and I'm his manager."

She looked at him scornfully. "Maybe you are. Go out an' tell that to Lud Fuller. If you get back to town alive, I'll be inclined to believe you."

"Thank you, Ma'am," he smiled at her. "I shall look forward to seeing you when you've decided I'm not a liar. I sure hate to have such a right pretty girl think so hard of me."

He turned and walked out and Ben Otten looked after him, mightily puzzled. There was a quality about him . . . Otten was reminded vaguely of something. For an instant there, as the man spoke and then as he turned away, Otten had seemed to smell the dust of another cowtown street, the sound of boot heels on a walk; but then the memory was gone, and he saw Mary Blake turn on him again. He braced himself to meet her anger.

It was strangely lacking. "Who is he, Ben? Where did he come from?"

Otten picked up the letters and stacked them together. "His credentials are in order, Mary. Joe Neal is alive. At least," he amended, "he was alive when these papers were signed. Nobody in this world could duplicate Joe Neal's scrawl. And those witnesses are names to swear by."

"But who is he?" she persisted.

"His name is Michael Blaine. I reckon we'll just have to wait and see who he is. Names, Mary," he added, "don't account for much. Not out here. It's

20

action that tells you who a man is. We'll see what kind of tracks he makes."

"Mighty small ones after he meets Lud. I'll bank on that."

Otten fumbled the papers into the envelope. That faint intangible memory was with him again. It caused him to say, "Don't be too sure, Mary. Never judge a man until he's showed himself. Unless I miss my guess, that man has smelled gunsmoke."

Gunsmoke! That was it! The day that Hickok killed Phil Coe in Abilene! That was the day. But why should it remind him of this? This man was not Hickok, and Coe was dead.

The afternoon was blistering hot. Utah squinted his eyes against the sun and walked up the street. By now the two loafers at the livery stable would have started their story. By now all eyes would be looking at him with speculation. Yet it was unlikely that anybody in Red Creek would know him. Most of these people had been around for several years. This was a settled community and not a trail town or a wide-open mining camp. They would have heard of Utah Blaine. But there was very little chance they would guess who he was—for awhile.

He carried his new saddlebags in his left hand and he walked up to the hotel and pushed open the door of the long lobby. The clerk turned and looked at him from under the rim of an eyeshade. Stepping up to the desk the clerk turned the register. "Twelve," he said, "at the end of the hall upstairs."

Blaine pulled the register closer and wrote in a quick, sure hand, *Michael J. Blaine, El Paso, Tex.*

The clerk glanced at it, then looked up. "Be with us long, Mr. Blaine?"

Blaine permitted himself a smile. "There seems to be a difference of opinion on that subject. But I'll tell you—I'll be here a lot longer than some of them that figuré otherwise."

He took his saddlebags and went up the steps. Inside the room he doffed his coat, placed the new six-shooter on the table beside him and proceeded to bathe and shave. As he dressed again, his thoughts returned to the girl. She was something, a real beauty. He grinned as he recalled her quick challenge and accusation. She had fire, too. Well, he liked a girl with spirit.

Glancing from the window he saw a man come out of the saloon across the street and stare up at the hotel. Then the man started across, little puffs of dust rising from his boots. He was a tall, slightly stooped man with unusually high heels. They gave him a queer, forward-leaning movement. He paused in the street and stared up again, something sinister in his fixed scrutiny.

Blaine turned from the window and opened the carpet bag he had brought with him. From it he took a pair of holsters and a wide gunbelt. He slung the belt around him and buckled it, then took from the bag two beautifully matched pistols. They were 44 Russians. He checked their loads, then played with them briefly, spinning them, doing a couple of rapid border shifts and then dropping them into their holsters. Suddenly his hands flashed and the guns were in his hands.

He returned the guns to their holsters and, with strips of rawhide, tied them down. Once again, despite the heat, he put on the black coat. There was a sudden hammering on the door.

"Come in," he said. "It isn't locked."

The door slammed back and the man from the

street stood in the doorway. He was even taller than Blaine, but he was stooped and his jaws were lean, his cheeks hollow. He stared at Blaine. "You ain't goin' to get away with it!" he flared. "I'm tellin' you now, stay away from the 46!"

"You have rights there?" Blaine asked gently.

"That's no affair of yours! We'll have no strangers hornin' in."

"My job is not to horn in," Blaine said. "I'm to manage the 46. That's just what I intend to do."

"Bah!" The man stepped further into the room. "Don't try to throw that guff on me! Lee Fox is no fool! Neal's dead, an' you damn' well know it! An' I ain't sorry, neither. He cornered that range when he first come into this country and he hung onto it. Now he's gone an' the rest of us have a chance. Believe you me, I'll get mine!"

"Fox," Blaine said it quietly, "regardless of what you may think or hope, I am manager of the 46 Connected. As such I will warn you now, and I shall not repeat it later, that I want none of your stock on 46 range. Nor do I want any branding of mavericks on our range. Every foot of it, every inch, is going to be held. Now that's settled."

"You think it's settled! Why, damn you, I—" His eyes caught the rawhide thongs about Blaine's legs and he hesitated, his voice changing abruptly, curiously. "Gunman, hey? Or do you just wear 'em for show? Better not be bluffin', because you'll get called."

"Fox," Blaine's voice was even and he was smiling a little, "I do bluff occasionally, but I can stand a call. Don't forget it. Any time you and anybody else want to call, they'll have sixes to beat."

CHAPTER III

THE STALLION was fretting in his stall when Utah came down to the stable the next morning. Saddling him up, he led the dun stallion outside and mounted; then he rode up to the eating house. Despite the early hour, two other horses were tied at the hitch rail before the cafe.

Both men looked up as he entered. One of them was a slender young fellow with an intelligent, attractive face. He had sharply cut features and clear gray eyes. He nodded to Utah. "How are you, Blaine? I recognized you from the descriptions." He held out his hand. "I'm Ralston Forbes. I own the local newspaper."

Blaine shook hands gravely. "First I've heard of a paper," he said. "You take ads?"

Forbes laughed. "You wouldn't ask that if you knew the business. Advertising is the lifeblood of the business."

"Then take one for me. Just say that Mike Blaine has taken the job of manager for the 46 Connected and in the absence of Joe Neal all business will be with him."

Forbes chuckled. "If I didn't need the dollar that ad will cost you, I'd run it as news, because it will be the worst news some of these ranchers have had in years. All of them liked Joe, but they liked his range better. In a free range country you know what that means."

"I know." Blaine was aware that a subtle warning was being conveyed by the editor. He also noticed that the other man was not saying anything, and that Forbes expected him to. However, they didn't have to wait much longer.

24

The man was short and blocky with a beefy red face and hard gray eyes. He stabbed a slab of beef and brought it to his plate. "Have your fun," he said, "while you're able. You won't last long."

Blaine shrugged. "Two ways to look at that."

"Not hereabouts. These folks don't take kindly to no brash stranger comin' in here tryin' to run a blazer on 'em. Joe Neal was hung. He got his neck stretched nigh two weeks ago."

Blaine's voice was soft. "Were you there, friend?"

The blue eyes blazed as the man turned his head slowly. "No. But I've got it on good authority that he was hung." He slapped butter on a stack of hot cakes. "I'll take that as true. The gent who told me should know."

"It wouldn't be Lud Fuller, would it?"

The man did not look around this time. He kept spreading butter. "What makes you mention Lud? He was Neal's foreman."

"I know that. I also know he was there." Blaine filled his cup again. "And, friend, I'll take an oath on that."

Both men stared at him. The only way he could swear to it would be if he saw it. If he had been there, in the vicinity. The short man shrugged it off and cut off a huge triangle of hot cakes and stuffed them in his mouth. When he could talk again, he said, "You go on out to the ranch. You tell that to Lud. Better have a gun in your hand when you do it, though. Lud's fast."

"Is he?" Blaine chuckled. "I've known a few fast men."

Rals Forbes was suddenly staring hard at him. He slammed his palm on the table. "I'm losing my mind," he said excitedly. "What's the matter with me? You're Utah Blaine!"

The stocky man dropped his fork and his mouth opened. He took a deep breath and swallowed, then slowly his tongue went over his lips. The feeling in his stomach was not pleasant. A tough man, he knew his limitations, and he did not rank anywhere near the man as Utah Blaine was reputed to be. Nor, he reflected, did Lud Fuller. There was only one man, maybe two, in all this country around who might have a show with him.

"That's right," Utah replied, "I'm that Blaine."

He got to his feet and Forbes walked to the door with him. There Forbes hesitated briefly and said, "By the way, Blaine, if you make this stick you could do me a favor. There's a girl homesteading on your range. Right back up against the mountains. Her name is Angela Kinyon. Joe let her stay there, so I hope you will."

"It's still Joe Neal's ranch."

Forbes looked at him carefully. "All right, leave it that way. Angie's all right. She's had a hard time, but she's all woman and a fine person. Just so she stays, it doesn't matter."

"She'll stay."

"And watch your step, Utah. Not even you could stop this bunch if they get started. Every man in this country has been poised and ready to jump at the 46 range. They'll have it, too. I doubt if even Joe's being alive will stop 'em now. They've wanted it too long, and this is the first excuse they've had. It would take a hard, gun-fighting outfit to hold it now, and even then it would be a question. One man could never do it."

"Any of that crowd that could be trusted?"

"I doubt it. When you ride onto 46 range, you ride alone."

Riding up the trail to the crest of the Tule Mesa, Utah Blaine rolled a cigarette while studying the country. His knowledge of this land might mean the difference between life and death, and he was too competent a fighting man not to devote time to a study of the terrain.

The trail went down off the mesa and into the coolness of a pine forest before cutting through some cedars and down into the valley itself. There were rich green meadows close along the streams, and along the streams there were cottonwoods, willows and sycamore trees. The ranch itself lay in a grove of trees, most of them giant sycamores.

Large and ancient, the ranch house occupied a small knoll among the trees with the barns and corrals below it. As Blaine rode up to the yard he saw a man come out of the bunkhouse with a roll of bedding under his arm and start up the hill toward the house. The sound of his horse stopped the man, who turned to stare at him.

Utah glanced once at the bunkhouse. Another man had come from the door and stood there leaning against the door jamb, a cigarette in his lips. Blaine walked his horse toward the man with the bedding. This, he rightly surmised, would be Lud Fuller.

Fuller was a big man, thick in the waist, but deep in chest and arms bulging with muscle. He was unshaven and had cold, cruel eyes.

Blaine drew up the horse and swung down, trailing the reins. "Are you Fuller?" he asked.

"What d' you want?" Fuller demanded.

Blaine smiled. "My name is Blaine. I'm the new manager of the outfit. If you're the foreman, we'll have business to discuss."

Fuller was astonished. Of all the things he might

27

have expected, this was certainly not one of them. It took him a minute to get the idea and when it got across to him he was furious. "You're what!" He dropped his bedding. "Look, stranger, I don't know what you've got in your skull, but if that's a sign of it, you're breedin' a mighty poor brand of humor."

"This is no joke, Fuller. Joe Neal appointed me manager. I've visited the bank and Otten agrees my papers are in order. You'd better take that bedding back to the bunkhouse—unless you're quitting."

"Quittin', hell!" Fuller stepped over his bedding. "Neal's dead, an' this here's a crooked deal!"

Blaine's eyes were cold. "No, Lud, Neal isn't dead. He is very much alive. Does that signature look like he was dead?"

Blaine handed the letter to Fuller who glared at it, too filled with fury and disappointment to speak. He was scarcely able to see. Yet the signature was there, and it was Joe Neal's. Nobody could ever write like that but Neal himself.

"You can't get away with this!" Fuller's voice was hoarse.

"I'm not trying to get away with anything, Fuller." Blaine kept his voice calm. "I've been given a job, and I've come to take over. From here out you'll be subject to my orders."

"Like hell!" Fuller snarled. "I'm boss here and I'll stay boss. There's something rotten about this!"

"You're exactly right. It's a rotten deal when a man's friends turn against him and try to hang him for nothing except that they want to steal his ranch. Now get this into your skull, Fuller. You take orders from me or get off the ranch! And you can start right now!"

Fuller was beyond reason. Unable to coordinate

28

his thoughts and realize what had happened, his one instinct was to fight, to strike out, to attack. Despite the fact that he had himself put the rope on Neal, he knew that signature was genuine. But this curbed none of his anger.

Men were coming from the bunkhouse. Only minutes before, Fuller had rolled his bedding and told them he was moving into the big house. They had looked at him, but said nothing. Like himself they wanted to get something out of this new situation. But most of them wanted to strip the ranch of cattle, sell them off and skip. They were men Fuller had hired himself, for Neal had left most of the hiring in his hands. Only Rip Coker had spoken up. He was a hatchet-faced cowhand, tough, blond and wicked. "I'd go slow if I were you," he had said, "the old man might show up."

"He won't."

"You seem mighty sure of that. Maybe you made sure he won't."

Fuller had glared, but something in him warned that Coker would be no easy task in a gun fight. With his hands—well, Lud Fuller had never been whipped with fists. But the lean, wiry Coker was not the man to fight with his hands. Therefore Fuller had merely turned and walked up the hill with his bedroll. Now he was stopped and he could hear them coming, Coker among them.

"Joe Neal," Fuller persisted, "is dead. I'm takin' over."

Blaine shook his head. "Sorry to tear down your dream house," he said, "but you're just a little previous. Get back to the bunkhouse with your bed or load up and get off the place."

Blaine turned to the seven men who had come up the hill. "I'm Blaine, the new manager here. I

29

have shown my papers to Fuller. Before that I showed them to Otten. They are in order. Any of you men who want to draw your time can have it. Any of you that want to stay, you have a job. Think it over. I'll see you at chuck."

Deliberately he turned his back and started up the hill to the house.

Fuller stared after him. "Hey! You!" he yelled.

Blaine kept on walking. Opening the door to the house, he stepped inside.

Rip Coker chuckled suddenly. "Looks like you should of took my advice, Lud. You jumped the gun."

"He won't get away with this!" Lud said furiously.

"Looks to me like he already has," Coker said. "Don't you try buckin' that hombre, Lud. He's out of your class."

Lud Fuller was too angry to listen. Slowly, the men turned. There was muttering among them, for several had already been spending the money they expected to get from the stolen cattle. Now it was over. Coker looked toward the house with a glint in his eyes; then he began to chuckle softly. The situation appealed to him. It had done him good to see the way Blaine turned Fuller off short. But what was to happen next?

Wiser than Fuller, Coker had complete appreciation of the situation in the Red Creek country. Fuller might grab the ranch, but he would never keep it. He was only one wolf among many who wanted this range; and his teeth were not sharp enough, his brain not keen enough. In this game of guns, grab and get, he would be out-grabbed and out-gunned.

Rip Coker rolled a smoke and squinted at the

30

blue hills. There would be some shuffling now. It seemed like one man against them all, and the odds appealed to Rip. He chuckled softly to himself.

Lud Fuller walked back to the bunkhouse and slammed his bedroll on the bunk. He glared right and left, looking for something on which he could take out his fury. Then he stalked outside and walked toward the corral. He would ride over and see Nevers. He would see Clell Miller, on the B-Bar. Something would have to be done about this and quick.

Coker watched him saddle up and ride out; then he turned and walked up the steps to the house. He was going to declare himself. As he reached for the door, Blaine pulled it open and stepped out. He had his coat off and he was wearing his two guns low. Rip Coker felt a little flicker of excitement go through him: this man was ready.

"My name's Coker," he said abruptly. "Been on this spread about four months. I'm the newest hand."

"All right, Coker. What's on your mind?"

"Looks like you're in for a scrap."

"I expected that."

"You're all alone."

"I expected that, too." Blaine grinned briefly. "Tell me something I don't know, friend."

Coker finished rolling his smoke. "Me," he said, without looking up. "I always was a sucker. I'm declaring myself in—on your side."

"Why?"

Coker's chuckle was dry. "Maybe because I'm just ornery an' like to buck a tough game. Maybe it's because I don't like fightin' with a gang. Maybe it's just because I want to be on your side when you're pushed."

"Those are all good reasons with me." Blaine

thrust out his hand. "Glad to have you with me, Coker. I won't warn you. You know the setup better than I do."

"I figure I do." Coker nodded toward the north. "Up there are about thirty land-hungry little ranchers. They are tougher'n boot leather, an' most of them have rustled a few head in their time. The B-Bar has a foreman named Clell Miller. He's a cousin of one of the old James' crowd and just as salty. He's a whiz with a six-gun and he'll tackle anything. He's figurin' on ownin' the B-Bar when the fight's over. And he figures on having added to it all that land between Skeleton Ridge and the river—which is 46 range."

"I see."

"Then see this. Ben Otten's friendly enough, a square man, but range hungry as the rest. If the thing breaks up, he'll come in grabbin' for his chunk of it."

"And the rest?"

"Fuller, Miller and Nevers are the worst."

"What about Lee Fox?"

Coker hesitated. "I don't figure him. He's poison mean, killed two of his hands about a year ago. Nobody figured him for a gun-slick, but when they braced him he came loose like a wildcat and he spit lead all over."

"Any others?"

"Uh huh. There's Rink Witter. He's Nevers' right hand."

"Heard of him."

"Figured you had. He's hell on wheels."

"How about these men to the north? Who's the big man up there?"

"Ortmann, and he's a hard man."

32

Blaine chuckled suddenly. "Sounds like I'm buckin' a stacked deck. You still want in?"

"You forget, I've known this all the time. Sure, I want in. I wouldn't miss it for the world!"

CHAPTER IV

MARY BLAKE swung down from her mare, stripped off the saddle and bridle, as she turned the horse into the corral. There was no one in sight when she started toward the house and she reflected bitterly that for all her father's training, she was not showing up so well as owner of a ranch. Not with a foreman like Clell Miller. But how could you fire such a man? She knew he would not go and she had no desire for a showdown until she was ready. Right now she had nothing to back her play. All she could do if he refused to go would be to shoot him from the house, and that went against the grain.

She felt lost, trapped. Two or three of the old hands would stand by her, she knew that. Kelsey and Timm would not fail her, and both were good men. But they were only two against so many, and she was too shrewd to risk them in a pointless struggle. They provided backing she had to keep in reserve until the likely moment came.

As she went up the steps, Miller came around the corner of the house. He was a tall, well-built man and good looking. He had a deep scar, all of three inches long, on one cheekbone. It was his brag that he had killed the man who put it there, and he liked to be asked about the incident.

"Back so soon?" His manner was elaborately polite. "Did Otten offer to send his men over to help?"

"I need no help."

He looked up at her impudently. "No? Well, maybe not. Looks to me like you're out on a limb."

She could see the danger of this sort of talk and swiftly changed the subject. "Joe Neal's alive."

Clell Miller had looked away. Now he swung his head back, swift passion flushing his face. "What was that? What did you say?"

"I said Joe Neal is alive."

"He's back in town?" Miller was incredulous, but had a lurking suspicion that she was telling the truth. Fury welled up within him. That damned Lud! Couldn't he do anything right?

"No, he's not back. He's in El Paso. He sent a manager down here. A man named Blaine."

"Blaine!" Miller's dark features sharpened suddenly and his eyes were those of an animal at bay. "What was his other name? What did they call him?"

Surprised at his excitement, she shrugged it off. "Why, his first name is Michael, I think. Do you know him?"

"Tall man? Broad shoulders? Green eyes?" Miller was tense with excitement.

"Why, yes. That sounds like him. Why, who is he?"

Miller stared at her, all his animosity toward her forgotten with this information. "Who?" he laughed shortly. "He's Utah Blaine, that's who he is, that hell-on-wheels gunman from the Neuces, the man who tamed Alta. He's killed twenty men, maybe thirty. Where did Neal round *him* up?"

Utah Blaine! She had heard her father talk of him so much that his name had been a legend to her. Mary remembered her father had been driving north right ahead of Shanghai Pierce's big herd

34

when Utah was trail boss. Gid Blake had been stopped by herd cutters and she knew every word of that story from memory, how Blaine had faced them down, killed their fastest gunfighter, and told them to break up and scatter. Her father had gone through without trouble, although at first he was sure he was going to lose cattle. Somehow she had expected Utah Blaine to be an older man. It was strangely exciting to realize that her girlhood hero was here, taking over the 46 Connected.

Clell Miller was excited and for the moment he had forgotten his troubles. Miller had never faced a gunfighter of top skill, but he knew that many rated him right along with them. There were those who said he was faster than Hardin. But he knew nobody was faster than Hardin, not anybody at all. Nevertheless, it would be something to kill Blaine! Something inside him leaped at the thought. To be the man who killed Utah Blaine! He walked off without a further word, bursting with excitement and the desire to talk.

Mary went on up the steps and closed the door carefully behind her before crossing the porch. When she entered the large room decorated with Navajo blankets the first person she saw was Tom Kelsey. He got up quickly and stepped toward her. He was a solid, square-built man, a top hand in any crowd, and he was, she knew, in love with her—not that he expected anything to come from it.

"Ma'am," he said quickly, "I think Miller's fixin' to drive off some cows. He's got maybe a hundred head bunched in Canyon Creek."

"Where's Dan Timm?"

"He's watchin' 'em, Ma'am. We figured I'd best come back an' tell you."

"Thanks, Tom, but there's nothing we can do. Not right now, anyway. We'll have to let it ride. We can't risk a showdown."

Tom Kelsey twisted his hat in his fingers. This he knew perfectly well, but it griped him. He wanted to do something. But while a fair hand with a gun, he was not in Clell Miller's class and knew it. Nevertheless, to let him get away without a fight went against the grain.

"We may have a chance now, Tom. I want you to do something for me. Ride back and get Timm. Send him to me. I want one of you to stay in this house from now on. I don't trust Clell or any of that crowd. But after you have started Timm back, I want you to ride on over to the 46. Utah Blaine is there."

"Are you sure? What's he want there?"

She explained, her eyes watching the bunkhouse through the window. "I want you to tell him I want to see him. And talk to him alone."

When he had gone she walked into her own room and began to comb her hair. She was a slim, boyish girl with beautiful eyes and lips. Her figure, while only beginning to take on the shape another year or two would give her, was still very good. She looked at herself in the mirror, her not too thin lips, good shoulders and nice throat and chin.

For the first time since her father's murder she thought she saw a way out. She had Timm and Kelsey. If they could get together with Blaine, they would have the beginning of a fighting outfit. Not enough, but such a man as Blaine was a man to build around.

As Mary Blake pondered the problem of concerted action against those who would split up the range of the two large outfits, Lud Fuller was whipping a foam-flecked horse down the trail to the Big N outfit of Russ Nevers.

Within him burned a dull rage that defied all reason. Joe Neal, whom he had hated during all the time he worked for him, was alive! He did not stop to think how he was alive, or what had happened—all he could think of was that fact. Not even the appearance of Blaine had hit him as hard.

His hatred for Neal was not born of any wrong Neal had done him, for Neal had always been strictly fair with his men, his foreman included. That hatred was something that had grown from deep within the fiber of the man himself, some deeply hidden store of bile born of envy, jealousy, and a hatred for all that seemed above him.

To any other man but Lud the grievances would have been trivial things but during long hours in the saddle or lying on his bunk, Lud's slow mind mulled over them and they grew into festering hatred and resentment.

Nevers looked up as Lud rode into the ranch yard. "Neal's alive!" Fuller burst out, his eyes bulging. "He ain't dead! He sent a man—"

"Shut up, you fool!" Nevers stepped toward him, his voice cracking and harsh. "Shut that big mouth! I know all about it! What I want to know is what you're doin' here? Roust out your damned vigilantes now and hang him!"

"Neal?" Fuller asked stupidly.

"No, you fool! Blaine." Angrily he stared at the big foreman. "Don't stand there like a fool! Get busy! Let him alone for a few days and he'll get set. Hang him! Hang him now! His rep is bad enough so there'll be an excuse! Get busy!"

Lud Fuller was half way back to the ranch before he began to get angry at Nevers.

CHAPTER V

ALL THE HANDS were at table when Utah Blaine walked in and seated himself. He felt like hell and didn't care who knew. He hated checking over books and that was what he had been doing for half the night. The first thing, of course, was to find out just what it was he was managing, and he discovered it was plenty.

Thirty thousand head, Joe Neal had said. Well, the ranch would carry more, and some of those were ready to sell. It was time the ranch was worked over but good. There was water and there was grass. He considered that with a cold, clear brain and liked what he decided. It was time some new elements were injected into this game.

Coker had stated it clearly the night before, and he decided he liked Coker. Also, there had been that talk with Tom Kelsey. Mary Blake wanted to talk to him, but she had little to offer. Kelsey had said she had two loyal hands. Still, that made four of them if they worked together, and Kelsey, while not as salty as Rip Coker, was a solid man. The sort that would have staying power. He would talk to Mary Blake.

Lud Fuller was there, his big jaw swinging up and down as he chomped his food. "Lud," Blaine said, "there's a lot to be done on this outfit. Take four men and head for Squaw Peak. There will be some of our stuff up there. I want everything wearing our brand thrown back across the river."

Fuller started to object angrily. Squaw Peak? Why, that was away north! There would be no chance for him to organize any vigilante meeting up there! He started to object, but the logic of the move appealed to him. Those nesters were always cutting out 46 stock and butchering it.

"You givin' up that range?" he looked up from his plate.

"I'm givin' up nothing. From what I hear Ortmann an' his boys up there are makin' mighty free with our stock. Well, we'll throw our beef back across the river until we get a chance to clean them out of there."

All eyes were on him. "We'll clean them out," he said, "or make believers of them."

"That's a sizeable job," the speaker was a long-geared man with sparse red hair. "They'll fight."

"I've tackled sizeable jobs before," Blaine said shortly, "and they fought."

There was no answer to that for they all knew the story of the mining town of Alta where three marshals had lasted a day each, and then Utah Blaine rode in and took the job. Four men had died the first week he was on the job. The leader of the bad ones going first, on the first night. Twenty-two men had been jailed that night, and two had gone to the one-room hospital with cracked skulls.

Alta, where there had been a killing every night, and where sixty-two men had been buried in Boot Hill before one townsman died of natural causes. The town where there were seven thousand belted men headed straight for the doors of Hell, and every one of them packing a gun. Two thousand miners and five thousand to rob them—and Blaine had tamed the town. It was there they started calling him Utah.

"Like I said," he continued, "take your men and

move up there. Work well back up in all the draws. No stock but our own, but start it for the river. Nobody works alone, work two or three together and hit both heads of Chasm Creek. Check the head of Gap mighty careful because I've an idea when they take our beef it goes over from Gap into Chalktank. Then work south. It will be slow, but throw the beef back over the river."

"You aim to talk to Ortmann?" Red asked.

"When I'm ready."

The other hands waited expectantly. "Coker, there's a busted stall in the barn and that corral needs work. That's for you." He looked beyond the hatchet-faced warrior. "The rest of you work south along the edge of the mesa to Skeleton Ridge. You do the same thing. Throw the cattle back across the river!"

He finished eating and took a final swallow of coffee. Abruptly, he got to his feet. As he picked up his hat, he let his eyes go over the crowd. "I'm new here. New to you and you're new to me. If any of you ever have any kick coming, you come and make it. But get this between your ears. I'm runnin' the 46 and I'm goin' to run it smooth. If it gets rough, then I'll smooth her out. You boys won't have any trouble as long as you do your jobs."

He stepped out and closed the door behind him. Coker stuffed his mouth with a chunk of beef to keep from laughing. Fuller was flabbergasted. Obviously, he didn't know what to do. As poor a foreman as he was, he knew sensible orders when he heard them. Throwing the cattle back across the river would undoubtedly save a good many head from rustlers. From the ranch house a man with a glass could watch the river, and see the whole length

40

of it as it crossed the range. Nobody could possibly drive off cattle which were to the ranch side of the river.

Coker could see the idea penetrating Fuller's thick skull and could see Fuller's grudging appreciation of the tactics it implied. Coker could also see that Blaine's promise to face Ortmann had aroused the men's admiration. Moreover, what Blaine had done most successfully was to take the play away from them. Fuller had to obey orders or be fired. Once off the range Fuller was useless to the others and they would cut him out of the gang that expected to split the spoils of the ranch. Fuller was shrewd enough to appreciate all this.

While Coker disliked the work around the ranch, he also appreciated that Blaine was keeping the one man he could trust close at hand.

As soon as Fuller had left him, Nevers saddled up and rode for the B-Bar. He met Clell Miller when he was halfway there. Clell pulled up his sweating horse.

"Lud played hell!" Nevers burst out. "Neal's alive, and now when this Blaine shows up he runs to me instead of doin' somethin' about it."

Miller curled his leg around the saddle-horn. "What you aim to do, Nevers?"

"I ain't goin' to see no outsider jump that range!"

"You think Neal is dead?"

"How should I know? If he ain't, he's gonna be, believe you me!"

Miller looked at Nevers thoughtfully. "That's an idea," he said, "a good idea."

"Look," Nevers came closer, "Neal may or may not be alive. If he's dead, we've got to know it. If he's

41

alive, he's got to be killed. I ain't gonna be cheated at this stage of the game."

"Blaine ain't no cinch," Miller said.

"Afraid?"

"You know better than that."

Nevers nodded. "Yeah, I do. Forget it. I'm jumpy myself."

"What about Neal?"

"Don't let it bother you. Just you think about Blaine."

Clell Miller looked down at the older man. So that was the way it was? You never knew about a man until you got into a deal with him. This was a steal. Miller was making no bones about that with himself, and he would not hesitate to kill if somebody got in the way. But everybody knew what he was and who he was. However, they had never exactly known about Nevers. They thought they knew, but . . . Miller got out the makin's. "Where's Rink?"

"Never you mind about Rink. He's got his own work to do."

So that was it! Rink had gone after the old man, Joe Neal. Well, there wasn't a better man for the job. Little leather-faced Rink with his cold eyes and his remorseless way. A fast hand with a gun and ready to kill—a sure-thing operator. He would make no mistakes.

That meant the 46 Connected range was going to be thrown to the wolves, all right. "What about Blaine?" he insisted. "What if he won't stand still for it?"

"He won't have to," Nevers said. "We're going after Blaine. We're going to corner him. No gunfights, Clell. We can't take the risk. We're all going in. You, me, Lud—all of us."

"Otten?"

"Otten's out of it. I mean, he will be after we do all the dirty work. If he tries to get in we'll cut him off at the pockets. Far's that goes, we might as well split his range too if he gets ornery."

Clell Miller looked thoughtfully at the end of his cigarette. Nevers was like a bull. Once started nothing would stop him. Clell considered the matter. With anyone but Blaine the steal would seem like a cinch. "Why don't we steer Blaine into Ortmann?" he suggested. "Let 'em kill each other off?"

"Too slow." Nevers liked the idea, though. Clell could see that. "But we might try it. Get rid of one of them, anyway. If he uses guns, Blaine will kill him. If Ortmann ever got his hands on Blaine it would be the end of Utah."

"He'd never let him. Blaine's no fool."

"Get your boys together," Nevers advised. "I'll put a bug in Ortmann's ear. Maybe we can get them together. If we don't succeed we'll move in fast. Your outfit and my outfit, and we'll pour cattle all over that range and hit Blaine from every direction at once. We'll cut him out of the herd, get him alone, and then kill him."

"What about Mary Blake?"

"Settle that when this is over. She's nothing to worry about."

"A couple of the boys will side her: Kelsey and Timm."

"Kill 'em. Get them out of it tonight. You hear, Clell?"

Riding back to the ranch, Clell considered that. Nevers was right. There was no use giving them a chance to side her. Get them now. Kelsey was a good man. Too good a man to die, yet that was the way it had to be.

With Lud out of the way, Blaine left Coker in charge and rode swiftly to meet with Mary Blake. The place of the meeting was designated as a spot called Goat Camp, beyond the river. As he neared the Bench, Utah glimpsed a spot of green back under the very shadow of the cliff. There, among some ancient cottonwoods and sycamores was a small cabin. With sharpening curiosity he realized this must be the cabin of the girl, Angie Kinyon.

He glanced at the sun. There was time for him to see Angie. He swung the horse from the trail. Before he reached the house, he saw the flowers. The place was literally banked with them, and he looked around with real pleasure. The house was shadowed by the cliff and the giant trees, and a small stream trickled past the house. Alongside the house were several fenced patches of crops. All showed careful attention and considerable appreciation for beauty as well as necessity. He rode up under the trees and swung down.

A door slammed behind him and he turned. The girl had stopped on the steps, a girl with dark hair and large soft dark eyes. She came down the steps quickly and he swept off his hat. "I'm Blaine," he said, "the manager of the 46. You'd be Angie Kinyon."

She gave him sharp attention, seeming to measure and gauge him in one swift, comprehensive glance. "I hadn't heard there was a manager."

He explained, taking his time and enjoying the coolness after the heat of his ride. She was a tall girl, but beautifully formed, and her voice was low and throaty. As he talked, he wondered at her presence in this far place.

"You've a beautiful place." There was a note of

wistfulness in his voice. "You must have been here quite awhile."

"Three years. It doesn't seem long."

She watched him, all her womanly curiosity turned upon this tall young man with the grave face and the slow smile. She had noted the two tied-down guns. She was far too knowing not to realize what they meant. Immediately she connected them with his name. She also knew better than most what an impact his presence must be making on the valley ranchers and their riders. Long before Joe Neal had any warning of what was coming, she had tried to warn him. She had watched the cattle of the 46 fattening on the rich graze and plentiful water, and she had seen the men from other ranches lingering hungrily around the edges. Their range was not bad, but it is not in many men to be satisfied with less than the best—when the best seems available.

Angie told Blaine this, of how stubborn Joe Neal was. He had wrested his range out of Apache country. Nobody would chase him from it.

"He told me he came here in '60," Blaine marveled. "How did he get along with the Indians? Surely there were a lot of them?"

"He talked peace when he could, fought when he had to. Twice all his men deserted but one, but he stayed on and fought it out."

"One stayed?"

"Yes." Angie Kinyon turned and indicated a stone slab at the head of a mound of earth under the sycamores some thirty yards away. There were flowers on the grave. "He lies there. He was my father."

"Oh." Utah looked at her curiously, this tall, lonely girl with the leaf shadows on her face. "You were here? Through all that?"

"My mother died in Texas before we came West

45

with Joe. I grew up here, through it all. Never a week went by that first year without a raid of some kind. The second year there were only three. Then there were years of peace, then more fighting as the Apache began to fear the soldiers and wanted to kill all white people."

"You never left?"

She looked at him quickly. "Then they haven't told you about me?"

"No. They told me nothing. Forbes told me you lived here."

"You've seen him?" The quick smile on her lips brought Utah a sharp twinge of jealousy that surprised him. Was that it, then? Was she in love with Forbes? "He's fine. One of the finest people I've known."

She was silent for a few minutes and he began thinking of his meeting at Goat Camp. "I'd better go."

She followed him. "Be careful." She put her hand on his sleeve suddenly. "Utah—do be careful! They'll all be after you, every one of them. There's not one you can trust."

"Maybe we can work something out. Mary Blake has two good men, and Coker is going to stand with me."

"Mary . . . then you've met her." Her eyes searched his face. "You're going to meet her now."

"Yes. To work out a plan of battle."

"She's selfish." She said it quickly and it surprised him. He had not expected her to speak ill of another woman. "She's been spoiled."

"I wouldn't know." Despite himself his voice was cool. "She only seems to want to protect her ranch."

Angie nodded seriously. "You didn't like what I said, did you? Perhaps I should only have said something nice. It would have been wiser for me, but of no use to you." When he did not respond, she added, "Mary is lovely, and she is like her father. Nothing existed in this world but the B-Bar for Gid. Mary is the same way. She is strong, too. They are underrating her, all of them. To keep that ranch intact she will lie, steal and kill."

"You really think that, don't you?" He put a foot in the stirrup and swung up. "Sometimes one has to kill."

She acknowledged that. "There are ways of killing. But remember what I have said. If she thought she could save the B-Bar by selling you out she would do it without hesitation."

He turned the dun stallion. "Well, thanks," he said, "but I think you judge her too severely."

"Perhaps." Her eyes were large and dark. She stood there in her buckskin skirt and calico blouse, looking lonely, beautiful, and sad. "I would not have said that, Utah Blaine, but I know the man you are, and I know you ride for Joe Neal, and for something stronger and better than all of them."

She turned abruptly and started for the house and he looked after her, a little puzzled, but captured by her grace. She turned suddenly, "When it happens that they are all against you," she said, "and it will happen so for I know them and they are wolves . . . when it happens, come to me. I will stand beside you as my father did beside Joe Neal."

CHAPTER VI

MARY BLAKE was waiting impatiently beside a spring at Goat Camp. There was nothing there but a dark and gloomy hut with a roof so sunken that only a midget could have used the old cabin. A stone corral and a shed thatched with branches loomed in the background.

She walked to Blaine quickly as he came up. "You're late. You've been talking to that girl."

"Angie? Yes, I have."

"She's beautiful." Mary said it shortly and Utah repressed a grin as he swung down. No love lost here, that was certain.

"Yes," he agreed cheerfully, "I believe she is. Now what's this proposition?"

"You may have guessed. I've two good men. Kelsey and Timm. Neither are gunmen but both will stick. They'll fight, too, and both are tough men. You have yourself. Together we can make a better fight than alone, and you—well, your name should draw some help to us."

"I've one man," he admitted, "Rip Coker."

She was immediately pleased. "Good! Oh, fine! He's the best of that lot on the 46, and as a fighting man he's worth two of my men. Good. And we can get some more. There's lots of them drifting into the Junction."

"Not them. Paid warriors."

"Aren't they all? Aren't you?" She flared at him, then she swept off her hat and shook out her hair. "Don't mind me, Utah, I'm upset by this thing. I'm snapping at everyone."

"It's understandable. I get a little upset at times."

She looked at him critically. "I doubt that. Were you ever upset by anything? Or anyone? You look too damnably self-sufficient, like you had ice water in your veins."

"All right," he brushed off her comments. "We've got four men and they had, as you suggest, better

48

perate together. The 46 is the center, and we could fort up there."

Her face changed swiftly. "And leave the B-Bar? Not for a minute. I thought you'd come over to my place. I could cook and I have Maria, too. I couldn't leave her alone."

You mean you couldn't leave the ranch alone, he told himself, then immediately felt guilty. After all his irritation at Angie he was adopting her viewpoint. "What we had better do," he said, "is ride into town and have a showdown with Otten. Swing him to our side."

"It won't work. He can gain nothing that way. He'll stay neutral as long as he can, then join them." She moved closer to him. "Utah, help me. On the 46 you'll have Ortmann on one side and the others to your south. You'll be between two fires. Come to the B-Bar and we can present a united front, with only enemies from one direction."

There was some logic in that, but not much. His own desire was to move right in, to take the bull by the horns. He said finally, "Tomorrow I'm riding to see Ortmann. I'm going to talk him out of this if I can, then I'll tackle the others."

"He won't listen to you."

"He'll have his chance."

She shrugged, then smiled at him. "Oh, I shouldn't argue! You're probably right. Only . . . only . . . only I'd feel safer if you were over there with me. Maria is wonderful, and I know she would die for me, and so would Kelsey and Timm, but neither of them could face Clell. He frightens me."

He looked at her quickly. "You don't think he'd bother you?"

"I wouldn't put it past him. Or the others." She was not being honest and she knew it. Clell—well, he might—but she doubted it. He liked telling her off, he liked being impudent because she had been boss so long, but Clell for all his killing and the innate vicious streak he undoubtedly had, was always respectful to women. Even, she had heard, to bad women.

Yet she could see her suggestion had influenced Utah. He was disturbed, and she set herself to play upon this advantage. He was handsome, she told herself. And the first man she had ever seen whom she could really admire. It would be pleasant to have him at the ranch.

"It seems so silly," she said, "you and Rip Coker down there batching when you could be having your meals with us. I can cook and so can Maria. And you know how foolish it is to divide our forces."

"I'll see Ortmann first," he said. "Then I'll come back this way and I'll bring Coker."

They left it at that.

All was quiet on the ranch when Blaine rode in, and none of the men were back. Rip walked out from the house with a Winchester in the crook of his arm. Briefly, Blaine explained the plan. Coker shrugged, "Well, it gives us some help we can use. I know those boys. One thing about them, they'll stick."

"All right," he said, "first thing tomorrow I'm heading for Ortmann's bunch. I'm going to try to swing him my way."

"You won't do it."

"We'll see, anyway. Want to come along?"

Coker chuckled. "I wouldn't miss it. I want to see your expression when you see that gent. He's bigger'n a horse, I tell you."

The next morning they were on their way. The trail led back to the rim of Tule Mesa and ran along the Mesa itself. It provided Blaine with a new chance to study the country and he took time to turn and look off to the southeast toward the Mazatzals, twenty-five miles away to the southeast. It was all that had been implied from the looks of it, a far and rugged country.

Rip rode without talking, his eyes always alert. They had reached the Yellowjacket Trail before he spoke.

"Neal's got me worried. What if something happens to him? I mean, what happens to you?"

It was a good question, and it started Utah thinking. He had come with the backing and authority of Neal, but if Neal died or was killed, he would be strictly on his own. His lips tightened at the thought. "No need to worry about that. Cross that bridge when we come to it."

"Better think of it." Coker shifted his seat in the saddle. "I'll bet Nevers has."

"What about Nevers? You know him?"

"Yep. He's one o' those gents who puts up an honest front but who's been mixed in a lot of dirty stuff. He's got guts, Utah, an' he's a wolf on the prowl, a hungry wolf. He's strong, tough, and smart. He's not erratic like Fox. He's no gunman, but he's been in a lot of fights. He'll be hard to handle."

Blaine shrugged and swung his horse into Yellowjacket Canyon. "None of them are easy."

Almost at once he saw the shacks. There were at least twenty of them. Not more than half of them were occupied, and the others were in varying stages of ruin. There was a long building with a porch on which was a sign that informed the wandering public that here was a saloon and store. Several loafers sat on the edge of the porch, legs dangling.

Blaine drew up. "Howdy, boys. Ortmann around?"

One of the men jerked his head. "Inside."

Utah dropped to the ground and Coker glanced at him, his eyes faintly amused. "I'll stand by," he said, "an' keep 'em off your back."

Utah grinned. "Keep 'em off yours," he retorted. Turning he walked up the steps. The loafers were all hardcases, he could see that. They eyed him wearily and glanced curiously at the hatchet-faced blond man who leaned against the watering trough.

There were three men inside the store and one of them was Lud Fuller.

Blaine stopped abruptly. "What you doin' over here, Lud?"

Fuller shifted his feet. He hadn't expected to meet Blaine and was confused. "Huntin' cows," he said bluntly.

"You'll find some back near the end of Chalktank," Blaine told him. "We rode past a few on the way up."

He turned then to look at the big man who sat on the counter. Blaine was to learn that Ortmann always sat on the counter because he had no chair to fit his huge size. He was the biggest man Blaine had ever seen, wide in the shoulder with a massive chest and huge hands. That he stood at least eight inches over six feet, Blaine could believe, and all his body was massive in proportion to his height.

"You're Blaine." Ortmann said it flatly and without emphasis.

"And you're Ortmann." Neither man made an effort to shake hands, but sized each other up coolly. Blaine's two hundred pounds of compact rangerider was dwarfed by the size of this man.

"I'm in a fight, Ortmann." Blaine had no intention of beating around the bush. "Neal is out of the state and I'm in charge here. It seems that everybody in this country has just been waitin' for a chance to grab off a chunk of 46 range."

"Includin' me," Ortmann acknowledged. His face was very wide and his jaw and cheekbones flat and heavy. He wore a short beard and his neck was a column of muscle coming from the homespun shirt. The chest was matted with hair.

"Includin' you," Blaine agreed. "But I'm goin' to win this fight, Ortmann, an' the fewer who get hurt the better. You," he said, "size up like a tough chunk of man. You've got some salty lads."

"You biddin' for our help?" Ortmann asked.

"I want no help. I'm askin' you to stay out. Let me handle the big outfits. I don't want you on my back while I'm tangling with the others."

"That's smart." Ortmann turned his glass in his fingers. He drank from a water glass and in his huge hand it looked like something a doll might use. "That's smart for you. Not so smart for me. That there range is free range. As long as a man uses it, he's got a rightful claim. When he steps out, it falls to him who can hold it. Well, me an' the boys want grass. We want plow-land. It lays there for us."

"No." Blaine's voice was cool. "You will never have one acre of that ground unless by permission from Joe Neal or myself. Not one acre. I say it here and now, and it will stick that way.

"Nor will anybody else. I'm saying that now and I hope you spread it around. All the ideas these would-be range grabbers have, they'd better forget. The 46 isn't givin' up anything."

"You talk mighty big. You ain't even got an outfit."

Utah Blaine did not smile. He did not move. He merely said quietly, "I'm my own outfit." Despite himself, Ortmann was impressed. "I don't need your help."

"In answer to your question." Ortmann got to his feet. "No, I won't lay off. Me an' the boys will move in whenever the time's ripe. You're through. The 46 is through. You ain't got a chance. The wolves will pull you down just like they pulled down Gid Blake."

Utah Blaine's eyes grew bleak and cold. "Have it your way, Ortmann," he said flatly. "But if that's the way you want it, the fight starts here."

For an instant the giant's eyes blinked. He was startled, and felt a reluctant admiration for this man. There was Ortmann, a giant unchallenged for strength and fighting fury. There were twenty of his men within call, and yet Blaine challenged him.

"You think you can kill me with that gun." Ortmann placed his big hands on his hips. "You might do it, but you'd never stop me before I got my hands on you. And then I'd kill you."

Blaine laughed harshly. "You think so?" He turned his head slightly. "Rip!" he yelled. "Come an' hold my coat! I'm goin' to whip the tallow out of this big moose!"

"Why, you damn' fool!" Fuller burst out. "He'll kill you!"

"You'd better hope he does," Blaine replied shortly. "I'll settle with you afterward."

As Coker came through the door, Blaine stripped off his guns and handed them to him. "Ortmann," he said, "my guns would stop you because every bullet would be in your heart. I can center every shot in the space of a dollar at a hundred yards. You'd be easy. But you're too good a man to kill, so I'm just goin' to whip you with my hands."

"Whip *me?*" Ortmann was incredulous.

"That's right." Utah Blaine grinned suddenly. He felt great. Something welled up inside of him, the fierce old love of battle that was never far from the surface. "You can be had, big boy. I'll bet you've never had a dozen fights in your life. You're too big. Well, I've had a hundred. Come on, you big lug, stack your duds and grease your skids. I'm goin' to tear down your meat house!"

Ortmann lunged, amazing swift for such a big man, but Utah's hands were up and he stabbed a jarring left to the teeth that flattened Ortmann's lips back. A lesser man would have been stopped in his tracks. It didn't even slow the giant.

One huge fist caught Blaine a jarring blow as he rolled to escape the punch. But with the same roll, he threw a right to the heart. It landed solidly, and flat-footed, feet wide apart, Utah rolled at the hips and hooked his left to Ortmann's belly. The punches landed hard and they hurt. Blaine went down in a half crouch and hooked a wide right that clipped Ortmann on the side of the head.

Ortmann stopped in his tracks and blinked. "You —you can hit!" he said, and lunged.

CHAPTER VII

ORTMANN punched swiftly, left and right. Utah slipped away from the left, but the right caught him in the chest and knocked him to the floor. Ortmann rushed him, but Blaine rolled over swiftly and came up, jarring against the counter as Ortmann closed in. Utah smashed a wicked short right to the belly and then a left. Burying his skull against the big man's chest, he began to swing in with both fists.

Ortmann got an arm around Blaine's body and held the punching left off. Then Ortmann smashed ponderously at Blaine's face. The blows thudded against cheekbone and skull and lights burst in Blaine's brain. Smashing down with the inside of his boot against Ortmann's shin, Blaine drove all his weight on the big man's instep. Ortmann let go with a yell and staggered back, and then Blaine hit him full.

Ortmann went back three full steps with Blaine closing in fast. But close against the counter the big man rolled aside and swung a left to the mouth and Blaine tasted blood. Wild with fury he drove at Ortmann, smashing with both fists, and Ortmann met him. Back they went. Ortmann suddenly reached out and grabbed Blaine by the arm and threw him against the door.

It swung back on its hinges and Blaine crashed through, off the porch and into the gray dust of the road. Following him, Ortmann sprang from the porch, his heels raised to crush the life from Utah. But swiftly Blaine had rolled over and staggered to his feet. He was more shaken than hurt. He blinked. Then as Ortmann hit the ground, momentarily off balance, Blaine swung. His fist flattened against Ortmann's nose and knocked him back against the porch. Crouched, Blaine stared at him through trickling sweat and blood. "How d' you like it, big fella?" he said, and walked in.

Ortmann ducked a left and smashed a right to Utah's ribs that stabbed pain into his vitals. He staggered back and fell, gasping wide-mouthed for air.

Ortmann came in and swung a heavy boot for his face. Blaine slapped it out of line and lunged upward, grabbing the big man in the crotch with one hand and by the shirt front with the other.

The momentum of Ortmann's rush and the pivot of Blaine's arms carried the big man off his feet and up high. Then Blaine threw him to the ground. Ortmann hit hard, and Blaine staggered back, glad for the momentary respite. Panting and mopping blood from his face, he watched the big man climb slowly to his feet.

Blaine had been wearing a skin tight glove on his left hand, and now he slipped another on his right, meanwhile watching the big man get up. Blaine's shirt was in rags and he ripped the few streamers of cloth away. His body was brown and powerful muscles rippled under the skin. He moved in, and Ortmann grinned at him. "Come on, little fella! Let's see you fight!"

Toe to toe they stood and slugged, smashing blows that were thrown with wicked power. Skull to skull they hit and battered. Ortmann's lips were pulp, a huge mouse was under one eye, almost closing it. There was a deep cut on Blaine's cheekbone and blood flowed continually. Inside his mouth there was a wicked cut.

Then Blaine stepped back suddenly. He caught Ortmann by the shoulder and pulled him forward, off balance. At the same time, he smashed a right to Ortmann's kidney.

Ortmann staggered, and Blaine moved quickly in and stabbed a swift left to the mouth. Then another. Then a hard driven left to the body followed by a right.

Blaine circled warily now, staying out of reach of those huge hands, away from that incredible weight. His legs felt leaden, his breath came in gasps. But he circled, then stepped in with a left to the head, and setting himself, smashed a right to the body. Ortmann went back a full step, his big head swaying like that of a drunken bear. Blaine moved in. He set himself and whipped that right to the body again, then a left and another right. Ortmann struck out feebly, and Blaine caught the wrist and threw Ortmann with a rolling hip-lock.

Ortmann got up slowly. His eyes were glazed, his face a smear of blood. He opened and closed his fingers, then started for Blaine. And Blaine came to meet him, low and hard, with a tackle around the knees. Ortmann tried to kick, but he was too slow. Blaine's shoulder struck and he went down. Quickly, Utah rolled free and got to his feet.

Ortmann got up, huge, indomitable, but whipped. Blaine backed off. "You're whipped, Ort," he said hoarsely, "don't make me hit you again."

"You wanted to fight," Ortmann said, "come on!"

"You're through," Blaine repeated. "From here on I'd cut you to ribbons, an' what would it prove? You're a tough man, an' you're game, but you're also licked."

Ortmann put a hand to his bloody face then stared at his fingers. He looked disgusted. "Why," he said, "I guess you're right!" He mopped at his face. Then he stared at Blaine, who was standing, bloody and battered, swaying on his feet, but ready. "You don't look so good yourself. Let's have a drink."

Arm in arm the two men staggered into the store and Ortmann got down a bottle and poured two big drinks, slopping the liquor on the counter. "Here," Blaine said, "is to a first class fightin' man!"

Ortmann lifted his glass, grinning with the good side of his mouth. They tossed off their drinks, and then Blaine turned abruptly to Lud Fuller who had followed them inside. "Lud, you're fired. Get your stuff off the place by sundown and you get out of the country. You tried to hang Joe Neal, tried to hang him slow so he'd strangle. You tried to double-cross me. If I see you after sundown tonight, I'll kill you!"

Lud's face grew ugly. "You talk big," he sneered, "for a man who ain't wearin' a gun! I've got a notion to—" his hand was on his gun.

"It's a bad notion, Lud," Rip Coker said, "but if you want to die, just try draggin' iron. Blaine ain't got a gun, but I have!"

Lud Fuller stared at Coker. The blond man's face was wicked in the dim light of the door. He stood lazily, hands hanging, but he was as ready as a crouching cougar. Fuller saw it and recognized what he saw. With a curse he swung out and walked from the room.

The return to the 46 was slow. Twice Blaine stopped and was sick. He had taken a wicked punch or two in the body and when he breathed a pain stabbed at his side. Rip Coker's eyes roved ceaselessly. "Wish Fuller had gone for his gun," he complained bitterly. "As long as he's alive he's a danger. He's yella, an' them kind worry me. They don't face up to a man. Not a bit."

Miles away, on the B-Bar, Timm paced restlessly while awaiting the return of Kelsey. He should have been back by now. Some of the crew were down in the bunkhouse and drunk. Where the liquor had come from he did not know, but he could guess. With Kelsey around he wouldn't be worried, but this was too big a house for one man to defend. Maria came in and brought him coffee. When

59

at last they heard a rattle of hoofs, Timm ran to the door. It was Mary.

"Gosh, Ma'am!" His voice shook. "I sure am glad to see you back! I been worried. Tom ain't showed up."

"Is Clell out there?"

"I don't figure so. He rode off an' I ain't seen him come back." Timm walked restlessly from window to window. "You better eat something. Did you see Blaine?"

"Yes. He's with us. And Rip Coker is with him."

That was good news to Timm. Utah's reputation was widely known, and while he knew little of Rip Coker, it was sufficient to know the man was a fighter. Nevertheless, knowing Tom Kelsey as he did, his continued absence worried him.

"When's Blaine showin' up?" he asked.

"He wanted to see Ortmann first. He thinks he can talk him out of butting in until the fight is over."

"Ma'am, where could Kelsey go? This ain't right. He was to start me back for here, which he done. Then he was to see Blaine. An' as Blaine met you, he sure enough did that—but where is he now?"

However, Tom Kelsey was not thinking of Timm. Nor was he thinking of getting back to the B-Bar. He was lying face down in the trail atop Mocking Bird Pass with three bullets in his body and his gun lying near his outflung hand.

Kelsey lay there in the road, his blood darkening the sand. A slow cool wind wound through the trees. Leaves stirred on the brush. His horse walked a few feet away, then looked back nervously, not liking the smell of blood. Then it walked into the thick green grass and began to crop grass. Kelsey did not move. The wind stirred the thin material on the back of his vest, moved his neckerchief.

Utah Blaine and Rip Coker found him there just at sundown. The best route from Yellowjacket to the B-Bar lay over 22 Mesa and through Mocking Bird. They switched horses at the Rice place on Sycamore. Rice was a lonely squatter who gardened a little, trapped a little, and broke a few wild horses he found in the canyon country. He was neutral and would always be. He took their horses without comment, glancing at Blaine's swollen and battered face with interest. But he asked no questions. "Take good care of that stallion," Blaine said. "I'll be back."

On fresh horses they pushed on, holding to a rapid gait. Things would begin to break fast now; they knew that. There was no time to be lost. Dusk was well along before they pushed into the Pass. Blaine was riding ahead when suddenly he reined in and palmed his gun. "Horse ahead," he said hoarsely. "No rider."

Rip grabbed his Winchester out of the bucket and spurred forward. Alert for an ambush, they glimpsed Kelsey's body almost at once. "Man down!" Rip said, and swung from the saddle. Then he swore.

"Who is it?" Blaine dropped to the ground.

"Kelsey. He's shot to doll rags. How he stayed alive this long, I don't know."

Blaine turned abruptly into a small copse and began breaking up dead dry branches. Swiftly, he built a fire. Making a square dish of birch bark, he began to boil water. Then he helped Coker carry the injured man to the fire. Coker stared at the bark container.

"Hell," he said, "why doesn't it burn? I never saw that before."

"Water absorbs the heat," Blaine explained. "Don't let the flames get above the water level. It's an Injun trick."

Working swiftly, they removed enough of Kelsey's clothes to get at the wounds. All were bad. Two were through the stomach and one right below the heart. There was, and both of them knew it, not once chance in a million.

Blaine bathed the wounds with hot water and then bandaged them. Kelsey stirred on the ground and then opened his eyes. "Blaine," he muttered. "Got to see Blaine."

"I'm here, Tom," Utah said. "Who shot you?"

"Blaine!" he groaned. "Blaine! You got to run! All of you! Get out! Mil—Miller told me. Neal's dead. Killed. They are all comin' after you."

Coker swore. Crouching over Kelsey's body, he demanded quickly, impatiently, "Tom—you sure?"

"Rink . . . Rink killed him."

"Rink," Coker straightened to his feet. "That tears it. If Rink went after Neal, then he's dead. That means you're out, Utah."

"Like hell." Utah was still working over the wounded man. "Take it easy, Tom."

"It ain't what you think I'm talkin' about," Coker protested. "It's them. With Neal dead you've no authority. The lid's off an' they'll come like locusts. An' they'll hunt you—us—like animals."

"Maybe." Utah's jaw was set, his face grim. Suddenly, he was tired. He had tried, but now Neal was dead. That good old man, murdered by Rink Witter.

Rink . . . well, that was something he could do. "I'll kill Rink," he said quietly.

"If you stay alive long enough." Coker was pacing the ground. "God, man. They'll all be after us! We'll have a real fight now!"

"Clell Miller did this?" Utah asked.

Kelsey was growing weaker. "Yes," he said faintly. "Don't mind me. I'm—I'm—finished. Ride. Get out."

He started a deep breath and never finished it.

Utah swore softly. "Good man gone," he said, unconsciously speaking his epitaph. "Let's get out of here. Timm will be alone at that ranch."

"Take his guns. We'll need 'em. I'll get his rifle and start his horse home."

They mounted again and rode off in silence, leaving behind them the body of a "good man gone."

When they crossed the ridge near Bloody Basin they could see, several miles off, the lights at the Big N.

"There they are," Coker said bitterly. "Gettin' ready for us."

Utah's comment was dry. "What you kickin' about? You asked for a fight."

"You stickin' it out?"

"Sure."

Coker smiled. This was his kind of man. "You got a partner," he said quietly. Then he added, "You take Rink. I want Clell."

CHAPTER VIII

RINK WITTER had come upon Neal at Congress Junction. Witter, under orders from Nevers, had started for El Paso to find and kill Joe Neal. He arrived at the Junction in time to see Joe Neal get down from a cattle train, and Witter swung down from his horse and walked up the platform. Neal did not see him until they were less than twenty feet apart.

"Hello, Joe," Rink Witter said, and shot him three times through the stomach. As the old man fell, Witter walked up to him, kicked away the hand that groped for a gun and shot Neal again, between the eyes. Then he walked unhurriedly to his horse, mounted and rode back to the Big N.

The news swept the country like wildfire. Neal was dead. Blaine, therefore, no longer had any authority. The few who had lagged now saw there was no longer any reason for delay. As one man they started to move. Nevers began at once to gather his forces. He wanted to be on the 46 range in force before any opposition could arrive. Then he could dictate terms.

Otten worried him none at all despite the man's political influence over the Territory. Nevers figured they could buy Otten off with a few square miles of range which he would accept rather than enter a free-for-all fight. There would be trouble with Ortmann, but with Clell and Fuller's men that could be handled. It was Lee Fox who worried Nevers—far more than he would have admitted.

Fox, at Table Mountain, was between Nevers and the bulk of the 46 range. Moreover, Fox was a highly volatile person, one whose depth or ability could not be gauged. He was given to sudden driving impulses, and reason had no part in them. If he went into one of his killing furies the range might be soaked with blood within the week.

Nevertheless, Nevers fully appreciated the strategic value of the accomplished fact. If he were sitting at Headquarters on the 46, his position would be strong and he could dictate terms. Moreover, because of his affiliation with the hands of the two big spreads, he far outnumbered the others.

When Clell Miller reached the ranch house on the 46 he found it almost deserted. A few of the hands were around and they told him that neither Utah nor Lud were around. Fuller and some of his men had been sent off to work the north range and had not returned. Rip Coker was riding with Blaine.

Clell considered that while he built a smoke. Coker was a tough hand. If he had decided to ride with Blaine, they would make a tough combination to buck. Alone he couldn't tackle them. He turned his horse and rode south, heading for the river and the easiest route to the Big N.

Clell Miller was a man at odds with himself. For the first time a killing was riding him hard. The memory of the falling of Tom Kelsey, and the memory of just how good a man Kelsey had been nagged at him and worried him. He could not shake it off, and that had never been true before. An old timer had told him just what would happen, and that was years ago. "You're fast with your guns, Clell," he had said. "But someday you'll shoot the wrong man an' you'll never rest easy again."

Hunching his shoulders against the chill, Miller stared bitterly into the darkness. The night seemed unusually cold, and suddenly he felt a sharp distaste for going back to the Big N, for seeing those hot, greedy eyes of Nevers, the dried-up, poison-mean face of Rink Witter.

Utah Blaine rode up to the B-Bar and swung down. Then he said to Rip, "We'll have a showdown with the crew, right now."

He walked swiftly to the bunkhouse. Coker heard Timm come to the door. "Stay where you are, Timm. We'll handle it." He walked after Blaine who threw open the door of the bunkhouse and stepped in.

Five men were there. The other hands were off somewhere. One of those was dead drunk and snoring on a bunk. The others looked up when Blaine stepped in. Coker followed and moved swiftly to the right.

"Showdown, men!" Blaine spoke crisply. "All cards on the table. Neal's been murdered by Rink Witter. Clell Miller has killed Tom Kelsey, shot him down up on the Mocking Bird. Now you declare yourselves. If you're with us, fine! If you're not, you ride off the ranch right this minute, just as you are. If you want to call, shuck your iron and let's see how many of you die game!"

Nobody moved. Not a man there but had used a gun. Not a man there but who had been in fights. So they knew this one, and they liked nothing about it. With those two men facing them even their numerical superiority would not help. Several men would die in those close quarters and none of them wanted to die. Each seemed to feel that Blaine was directing his full attention at him.

"Always wanted a shot at some of you," Coker said easily. "Suppose we settle this fight right now. If you boys want it, you can have it."

A short, squat man with a stubble of coarse beard and a bald head spoke. "We'll ride out. We ain't afeerd, but we ain't buckin' no stacked deck. Do we take our guns?"

Blaine laughed. "Why, sure! I'd never shoot an unarmed man an' some of you rannies may need killin'! Take 'em along, but remember this: if I ever see any one of you east of Copper Creek or north of Deadman again, he'd better be grabbin' iron when I see him."

"My sentiments," Coker agreed. "Any of you feel like takin' a hand right now? Utah figures we should give you an out. Me, I'd as soon open the pot right now."

The bald man stared at him. "You wait. You'll get yours. You ain't so salty."

"Want to freshen me up?" Coker invited. "I think we ought to shorten the odds right here."

The man would say no more, but a tall, lean man in long underwear looked at Blaine. "Don't I get to put on no pants?" his voice was plaintive."

"You look better that way. I said you ride the way you are. If you hate to lose your gear, blame it on double-crossin' your brand."

The men trooped out, taking the dead drunk with them. One after another they rounded up their horses, mounted and rode off. There were no parting yells, nothing.

Mary Blake was standing in the doorway. Timm got up from where he had been crouched by the window with his Winchester.

"Utah! You're back! I was so worried!" she cried.

"Seen Tom?" Timm asked quickly.

Blaine hesitated, feeling how well these men had known each other. "Tom won't be back," he said quietly. "Clell Miller killed him on Mocking Bird."

Timm swore softly. "I was afraid of that. He was a good man, Tom was." He rubbed a fumbling hand over his chin. "Rode together eight years, the two of us. I wish," he added, "I was a gunslinger."

"Don't worry," Coker promised, "I'll stake out that hide myself."

Blaine walked restlessly across the room. He had never liked being cooped up when a fight was coming. It was his nature to attack. Nor did he like the presence of the women. Bluntly, he explained the situation to Mary. "The stage for hesitation is over now," he said quietly, "and all the chips are down. You'd better go."

"And leave you to fight them alone?" she protested. "I'll not go."

"It would be better if you did," he told her. "We may have to leave here, fight somewhere else."

Coker took his rifle and went outside, moving off into the night, and heading away from the house. Timm walked out on the porch and stood there, lighting his pipe. He felt lost without Kelsey. It seemed impossible that Tom could be dead.

"Mary," Utah said it quietly, "I wish you would go. Red Creek if you like, or over east of here, to that Mormon settlement. You might be safer there. All hell's breakin' loose now."

She looked at him, her eyes serious. "What will you do? What can you do now? Against them all, I mean? And without the backing of Joe Neal's authority?"

He had been thinking of that. The murder of Neal cut the ground from beneath his feet. Neal had no heirs and so the range would go by default. He might, of course, claim it himself. Had he the fighting men to enforce such a claim, he might even make it stick. But he had no such men nor the money to pay them.

Nor could they hope to hold out long against the forces to be thrown against them. "We've got to get out." He said it reluctantly but positively. "We've got to move. We'd be foolish to try to hold them off for long, but I will try. If we fail, then we'll run."

Coker had come back to the door. "Riders headed this way. What do we do?"

Utah turned to the door. "Better ride out, Mary. This isn't going to be nice."

"Are you quitting?"

He laughed without humor. "You're the second to ask me that question in the last few hours. No, I'm not quitting. A man killed Joe Neal. Another man ordered it. I've a job to do."

Rip Coker was leaning against the corner of the house. He looked around as Blaine walked over to him. "Quite a bunch. Timm's bedded down by that stone well."

"All right. Hold your fire unless they open the ball. If they do, don't miss any shots."

"Who's goin' to miss?"

Utah Blaine walked slowly down the trail. The moon was up and the night was bright. As the riders neared they slowed their pace. Blaine moved forward. "All right, hold it up!"

They drew up, a solid rank of at least twenty men. "That you, Blaine?"

"Sure. Who'd you expect? You murdered Joe Neal."

There was a short, pregnant silence. Nevers replied, his rage stifled. "All right, so Neal's dead. That finishes you on this place."

"I'd not say so. If Neal had lived he might have fired me. As it is, he can't. I was given a job. Nobody has taken me off. I plan to stay."

"Don't be a fool!" Nevers burst out. "I've twenty men here! I'm takin' over this spread right now."

"I wouldn't bet on it," Blaine replied quietly, "an' if you do take over, Nevers, you'll have fewer men than you've got now. And also," he paused slightly, "I'll be back."

"Not if you die now."

Blaine lifted his voice. "Boys, you're backin' this gent. Let's see what kind of an Injun he is. Nevers, I'll take you right now, with any man you pick to side you. I'll take the two of you right here in the moonlight, Nevers. Come on, how much guts have you got?"

It was the last thing in the world that Nevers had expected. Moreover, it was the last thing he wanted. With nerve enough for most purposes, he had no stomach for facing a gunfighter of Blaine's reputation—not even with a man to help him. He knew, just as Blaine had known he would, that Blaine's first shot would be for him—and it wouldn't miss.

Yet he knew how much depended on courageous leadership. Men, particularly Western men, do not follow cowards. He had been fairly called, and his mind groped for a way out, an excuse.

"What's the matter, Nevers? Not ready to die?" Utah taunted. "Don't worry too much. My hands aren't in the best shape right now, an' you might have a chance." He was stalling for time, trying to turn their attack, or at least to dull its force. "They took quite a hammering yesterday when I whipped Ortmann."

"When you what?"

That was somebody back in the crowd, one of the silent riders who waited the outcome of this talk.

From off to the left, Rip Coker spoke up. He wanted them to know he was there, too. "That's right, boys. Blaine gave Ortmann the beating of his life. Called him right in his own place of business and whipped him good. Although," he added, "I'd say Ort put up one hell of a scrap."

"Did you hear that?" One rider was speaking to

another. "Utah Blaine whipped Ortmann—with his *fists!*"

"Wish you gents would make up your minds to die," Coker commented casually. "This here Colt shotgun is loadin' my arms down."

Rip Coker was carrying a Winchester, but he was well back. He knew all they could see was light on his barrel. A Colt revolving shotgun carried four shells and no man in his right mind likes to buck a shotgun. It was a shrewd comment, well calculated to inspire distaste for battle in that vague light.

"Yeah," Timm's voice came from the well coping. "You hombres make a right tempting target. This Spencer sure can't miss at this range!"

All was quiet. Nobody spoke for several minutes. Nevers held himself still, glad that attention was off him for the minute. He had no desire to meet Blaine with guns now or at any time, yet he knew of no easy way out of the situation he was in. He had been neatly and effectually out-guessed and it infuriated him. Moreover, with a kind of intuition he knew that the men behind him had lost their enthusiasm for the attack. Blaine was bad enough, but that shotgun . . . a blast from a shotgun did awful things to a man, and this gun held four shells. And there was the possibility of reloads before they could get to him.

The Spencer .56 was no bargain either.

"All right!" Blaine stepped forward suddenly, gauging their hesitancy correctly. "Show's over for tonight. You boys want this ranch, you take it the hard way. Let's start back."

Nevers found his voice. "All right," he said evenly, "we'll go. But come daylight, we'll be back."

"Why sure! Glad to have you!" Blaine was chuck-

71

ling. "Room enough on this place to bury the lot of you."

Slowly, those in the rear began to back off. None of them seemed anxious to push ahead. Reluctantly, stifling his frustration and fury, Nevers followed his retreating men.

Rip Coker walked over slowly. "It'll never be that close again," he said sincerely. "I had goose flesh all over me there for a minute."

"That shotgun remark was sheer genius, Rip," Blaine said.

Coker was pleased. "Just a trick idea. I sure wouldn't want to buck a shotgun in the dark."

"What's next?" Timm had walked up. "I was listenin' for Clell, but I don't think he was with this outfit."

"We wait for morning," Blaine said, "and just before daybreak we'll pull out."

"Helll" Rip said. "We've got 'em stopped now, why run?"

"The object," Blaine said, "of any war is to destroy your enemy's fighting force. With superior numbers and armament the British couldn't whip Washington because they couldn't pin him down. He always managed to pull out and leave them holding the bag. That's what we do now.

"They'll never own this ranch," he said, "or the 46 as long as we're alive and in the country. We can let 'em have it today, an' we can take it back when we want it!"

CHAPTER IX

AT DAYBREAK they started east. Mary Blake, accompanied by the fat Maria, was to ride to the Mor-

72

mon settlement. Later, they would return to Red Creek and do what might be done there toward retaining title to their land. Blaine, accompanied by Rip Coker and Timm, took to the rugged country to the south.

The sun was hot and the three rode steadily, circling deeper into the hills. With them they had three pack animals loaded with food and ammunition.

"Maverick Springs," Timm told them. "That's the best place for us. She's 'way back in the hills in mighty rugged country."

Blaine mopped the sweat from his face and squinted through the sunlight toward the west. From the top of the mesa they could see a long sweep of the valley and the river. Table Mountain was slightly north of west from them and they could see riders fording the river.

"Lee Fox," Coker said. "Nevers won't have it all his own way."

"Nevers' place is beyond, in Bloody Basin, if I recall," Blaine said thoughtfully. "I figure we ought to pay him a visit after we cache these supplies."

"Now you're talkin'!" Coker agreed.

"An' we'll make three separate caches. No use havin' all our eggs in one basket."

They turned down into the canyon back of Razorback and made one cache at the base of Cypress Butte. They rode on through the tall pines, the air seeming cooler in their shade. There was the smell of heat, though, and the smell of dust. They took their time, anticipating no pursuit and not eager to tire their horses. Blaine thought several times of the stallion. He missed the fine horse and would pick him up in the next few days.

They rode at last into a secluded glen shielded

on all sides by ranks of pines and aspens. Scattered among these were a few giant walnut trees. They were now close under the Mazatzals which Blaine had observed from the faraway rim of Tule Mesa.

At daybreak, they moved out following Tangle Creek up to the Basin where they found the Big N standing alone. The only man on the place was the cook, who came to the door with a rifle. Utah stopped. "Where's Nevers?"

Coker had been bringing up the rear and at the first glimpse of the cook he had turned his horse sharply left and circled behind the house while Blaine stalled.

"Ain't none o' your business!" The cook retorted harshly. "Who 're you?"

"Blaine's the name." Utah saw Coker slip from his horse and start toward the back side of the house. "You tell Nevers to stay off the 46 and the B-Bar or take the consequences."

"Tell him yourself!" The cook retorted. He was about to amplify his remarks when the sharp prod of a gun muzzle cut him off short.

"Lower that shotgun mighty easy," Coker said quietly. "You might miss but I can't."

The logic of this was evident to the cook. Gingerly he lowered the shotgun and Coker reached around and took it from his hands. "What you goin' to do to me?" the cook demanded.

"You?" Blaine laughed. "We've no fight with you, man. Get us some grub. We've had a long ride and we ate a light breakfast. You just tell Nevers we were here. If he tries to grab any piece of the 46 we'll burn him out right here. You tell him that."

"There's only three of you," the cook objected, going about fixing the meal. "You won't have a chance."

"Well," Coker said cheerfully, tipping back in his chair, "you can bet on this. If we go, our burials will come after that of Nevers. Take it from me."

Nevers was unhappy. His men had closed in on the B-Bar ranch house only to find it deserted and empty. He was no fool, and he knew that there would be no safety for him or for anyone else on either the B-Bar or the 46 as long as Blaine was alive and in the vicinity.

Clell Miller rode in, unshaven and surly. Nevers went to him quickly. "Where's Blaine? You seen him?"

"No." Miller dismounted wearily. "An' I don't want to."

"Losin' your nerve?" Nevers sneered.

Miller turned sharply around and Nevers stiffened. "No," Clell spoke slowly, "but I don't like this. It looked good, but I don't like it now."

Nevers could see the man was on the ragged edge and he knew better than to push him. "What happened?"

"I met Tom Kelsey up on Mocking Bird," he said, "an' killed him."

"Oh." Nevers had liked Kelsey himself, and at the same time had known the man stood between them and the possession of the B-Bar.

"Blaine got away," he said, "with Coker an' Timm."

"There'll be hell to pay then," Miller was gloomy. "Nevers, let's call it off. I'm sick of it."

"Call it off?" Nevers' rage returned. "Are you crazy? The biggest deal ever an' you want to call it off. Anyway," he added practically, "nobody could stop it now. Even if we backed down the rest of them wouldn't."

"That's right." Clell Miller studied Nevers. "I wonder what will happen to you for the Neal killin'."

Nevers jerked around. "I didn't kill him."

"Witter killed him at your orders. But now what? Neal had friends, Nevers. Friends down at Phoenix, friends in Tucson. Some of them will ask questions. Far as that goes, Neal told me one time he helped Virgil Earp out of a tight spot. The Earps stand by their friends. Look how they stuck with Doc Halliday."

Nevers shook himself irritably. Despite his bluster, he was worried. Had he gone too far? But no—this was no time to waver and it was too late to turn back—much too late.

He scowled at the thought, then shook himself impatiently. "We'll run Blaine down. We'll have him in no time."

"Think he'll wait for you to come after him?"

Nevers turned his large head. "What do you mean?"

"Just this. I think he'll hit us an' hit hard. Have you forgotten Alta? I haven't. And the bunch he tackled in Alta were so much tougher than most of our crowd there's no comparison."

They stood there, not liking any part of what they felt, knowing there was no way back. Yet there was no stopping. Nevers heard a scrape of heels behind him and he turned. One of his riders was standing not far away with a rifle in his hands. "Riders, boss, quite a bunch. Looks like Lee Fox."

"Fox." Nevers said it aloud. There was that, too.

A tall man rode up on a yellow buckskin. He pulled up sharply and looked around him. "Moved right in, Nevers? Well, you keep it. I'm headin' for the 46."

"Nobody's made any claim yet." Nevers held himself in. "I want the 46 an' part of the B-Bar. You can have the rest."

Fox smiled. It was not a pleasant smile. Nevers had the feeling that he had had before. This man was riding the borderline of insanity. "Got it all figured, have you? What about Ben Otten?"

"He's out of it."

"Tell him that. You've got to take him in or he'll go to Neal's friends."

Grudgingly, Nevers admitted this. Where all had been simple, now all was complication. Maybe Miller wasn't getting weak-kneed after all; maybe he was just getting smart. "Go on up to the 46," he said. "We can settle it later."

Fox did not move. "We can settle now if you like."

Nevers was a bulldog. His big head came up slowly and he stared at Fox. "That makes no sense, Fox. No sense in killin' ourselves off." He turned slowly. "Lud, open that keg of whiskey. We might as well celebrate."

Fuller got up heavily. He had been profoundly shocked by Blaine's swift and brutal cutting down of Ortmann. It was something long believed impossible, yet the slashing power of Utah's fists had been a shocking thing. It had been soon apparent to all that Blaine had been the faster of the two, and he had hit the harder. Despite Ortmann's huge size, his blows had shaken Utah. They had failed to keep him down. By his victory, Utah Blaine had seemed invincible, then on top of this he had fired Fuller and had told him to get out of the country.

Fuller had said nothing about the fight. The news was around though, and while the men gathered to empty the half of whiskey, talk swung to it. "Never would have believed it if I hadn't seen it," Fuller said.

All eyes turned to him. Miller stepped forward, quick with interest. "You *saw* it?"

"Yeah." Fuller straightened up from driving the spigot into the keg that sat on an outdoor table. "Blaine ruined him. He cut him down like you'd cut up a beef. Ortmann was rugged but he never had a chance."

There was silence, and then a cool voice interrupted: "Am I invited?"

They turned swiftly. Utah Blaine stood there, his feet apart, his green eyes hard and ready beneath the flat brim of his hat. Beyond him, still astride their horses, were Rip Coker and Timm. Each held a shotgun taken from the Big N.

Nevers' face turned crimson. "You? *Here?*" His voice was thick.

"Why, sure." Utah let his eyes go slowly from one to the other and finally settled on Lud Fuller. The face of the 46 foreman turned white. "Don't let it get you, Lud. I invited myself here. You still got time to leave the country. But don't let me meet with you again."

"What do you want?" Nevers demanded.

"Want? Why, I saw you fellas were openin' a keg so we thought we'd come down." Blaine turned his eyes slowly to Nevers. "You sure make a nice target through the sights of a Winchester, Nevers. I come darn near liquidatin' the stock of the Big N."

Nevers stared at Blaine, hatred swelling within him. Yet even as it mounted, a little voice of caution whispered that he should go slowly. This situation was shot through with death.

"Had my sights on Miller, too," Blaine said. "I sort of like the looks of you boys with my sight partin' your eyes. It's a right good feelin'. I might have shot Miller, but I promised him."

Clell's nerves were jumping. "Yeah? To who?"

"Me, Clell," Rip Coker was smiling wickedly. "I asked for you. I always figured you weren't as salty with that six-gun as you figured. An' when we tangle remember it ain't goin' to be like it was with Tom Kelsey. That was murder, Clell."

Clell glared, but his eyes shifted. Timm's glance met his and Clell felt a little shiver. That quiet man—square-faced, cool, calm, steady Timm—his eyes held a kind of hatred that Clell had never seen before.

"Kelsey an' me rode together for years, Clell," Timm said.

Blaine stepped forward and jerked the tin cup from Nevers' fingers. Then he filled it partly. Stepping back, he looked at Nevers. "I'm goin' to kill you, Nevers," he said quietly, "but not today. We're just visitin' today. I promised Coker that I wouldn't kill you today if he wouldn't tackle Miller."

He turned and walked back, handing the cup up to Timm, who took a swallow, then passed it to Rip. Coker laughed and emptied the cup. Utah Blaine walked back, his spurs jingling. Nobody spoke; the riders stood around, watching him. Clell felt a faint stir of reluctant admiration. This man had guts, he told himself.

Rightly, Blaine had gauged them well. No Western man in his right mind was going to try reaching for a gun when three armed men, two of them with ready rifles, covered him. One man Blaine was not sure about was Lee Fox. Fox was a man who might gamble. Yet even as Utah thought that his slanting eyes went to Coker.

Rip was watching Fox with care. Trust Rip to know where the danger lay.

"Yeah," Blaine said, "you've started the killing with two murders, Neal and Kelsey. Both were good men. The killing can stop there if you back up and get off this ranch and stay off it and the 46 Connected."

"If you think we'll do that," Nevers replied, "you're crazy!"

"We won't back up," Fox interjected.

Utah Blaine took another drink and then replaced the cup on the keg. He stepped back. "All right, boys, this goes for every man jack of you. Get off the two ranches by sundown or the war's on. We'll kill you wherever we find you and we'll hang any man who injures any one of us."

"You talk mighty big for such a small outfit."

"Want to try your hand right now, Nevers?" Blaine looked at him from under the brim of his hat.

"Plenty of time," Nevers said.

Utah swung into the saddle. "All right, we've told you. Now it's on your head."

Suddenly his gun sprang to his hand. "Drop your belts!" The words craked like a whip. "Drop 'em, an' no mistakes!"

As one man their hands leaped to the buckles and they let go their gunbelts. "All right," Blaine said. "Turn around!" They turned, and then Blaine said, "Now run! Last man gets a load of buckshot!"

As one man they sprang forward and raced for the draw, and wheeling their horses, the three rode out of the clearing and into the trail.

Hearing the horses' hoofs, Nevers braced to a stop and yelled, "Horses! Get after 'em! I'll give five hundred dollars for Blaine, dead or alive!"

CHAPTER X

TIMM LED OFF as they left the Basin. Instead of taking the trail for Mocking Bird Pass he swung west into the bed of Soda Springs Creek. Trusting Timm's knowledge of the country, Blaine trailed behind him with Coker bringing up the rear. They rode swiftly, confident their start would keep them ahead without killing their horses.

Timm swung suddenly west over a shelf of rock. He turned up over a saddle in the Mustangs and into a creek bottom. The creek was dry now. Ahead of them loomed the battlemented side of Turret Peak where Apaches had been trapped and captured long ago.

"Fox had me worried. I was afraid he wouldn't stampede." Coker's comment was in line with Blaine's own thoughts. "It'll set him wild."

"Yeah, we're on the run now for sure."

Timm had nothing to say. The older man studied the hills, selecting their route with infinite care, leaving as little trail as possible. They turned and doubled back, choosing rocky shelves of sand so deep their tracks were formless and shapeless, mingling with those of wild horses and of cattle.

"How far are we from Otten's place?" Blaine asked.

"Just a whoop and a holler." Timm turned in his saddle. His face looked strangely youthful now, and Blaine noticed the humor around his eyes. Timm was taking to this like a duck to water. It probably brought memories of old days of campaigning. "You want to go over there?"

"Sure. As long as we're ridin', let's drop in on him."

"That outfit will be runnin' us," Coker warned.

"I know that. So this may be our last and only chance to see Otten."

Luckily, the banker was at the ranch. He came out of the house when he saw them approaching, but his face shadowed when he identified them. "What are you doin' here, Blaine? You'd best ride on out of the country."

"You'd like that, wouldn't you?" Blaine watched Timm lead the horses to the trough. "We're not goin', Ben. We're stayin'. We're goin' to fight it out."

"Don't be a fool!" Ben Otten was more worried than angry. "Look, boys, you don't have a chance! The whole country's against you. I don't want to see any more killing. Ride on out. If you're broke, I'll stake you."

"No." Blaine's voice was flat. He looked at Otten with cool, hard eyes. "I don't like bein' pushed and I'm not going to run. If I have to die here, I will. But believe me, Ben, they'll bury some men along with me."

"That's no way to talk." Otten was worried. He came down from the steps. "Where's Mary? What happened to her?"

"She's over in the Mormon settlements. She'll be safe if she stays there."

"Where's Tom Kelsey?"

"Then you haven't heard? Clell Miller killed him. Joe Neal's dead, too."

Otten nodded. "I know that. I'm sorry about Tom. Neal should have stayed out while he had the chance."

Utah Blaine stared down at the banker, his opinion showing in his eyes. "Ben," he said frankly, "you've the look of a good man. I hate to see you running with this pack of coyotes! Soon's a man is down you all run in to snap and tear at him."

"That's a hell of a thing to say." Otten kicked dirt with his boot toe. "Where'd you come from?"

"The B-Bar. We faced up to Nevers and Fox over there. Stopped by to tell them what they were buckin'. That's why we stopped here, Ben. You know what this means, don't you?"

Otten looked up, his eyes granite hard. "What does what mean? You're not bluffin' me, Utah!"

"I never bluff, Ben." Blaine said it quietly and the older man felt a distinct chill. "I'm just tellin' you. Run with that pack and you're through. I'll run you out of the country."

Otten's face darkened and he stepped foward, so furious he could scarcely speak. "You!" he shouted. "You'll run me out! Why you ragged-tailed gunslinger! You're nothin' but a damned driftin' outlaw! You stay here an' I'll see you hung! Don't you come around here tellin' me!"

"I've told you." Blaine turned his back on him and gathered up the reins of his horse.

"Let's go, Utah." Timm's voice showed his worry. "They'll be right behind us."

Blaine swung into the leather and then turned, dropping his glance to Otten. "Make your choice, man. But make it right. You've done nothing against me yet, so don't start."

In a tight group, the three rode out of the yard and Ben Otten stared after them, his hand on his gun. Why, the man was insane! He was on the run and he talked like it was the other way around! He'd . . . ! Ben's fury trailed off and old stories came flooding back into his mind. This man, alone and without help, had walked into Alta and tamed the town.

Otten knew other stories, too. More than once he

had heard Gid Blake's story of the trail cutters. He shook himself irritably, and swore aloud, then said, "Why, the man doesn't have a chance!" But the words rang hollow in his ears and he stared gloomily after them. Suppose the man did win? The answer to that was in Blaine's words: he never bluffed. He would do what he promised.

But that was absurd. Utah Blaine wouldn't last the week out. A few minutes later when Nevers and his hard-riding crew raced in, he became even more confident. It was not until he lay in bed that night that he remembered Blaine's face. He remembered those level green eyes and something turned over in him and left him cold and afraid.

Now the chase began. To the three riders it became grim and desperate. After nightfall they came down to the Rice cabin and after looking through the windows, tapped gently on the door.

"Who is it?" Rice demanded.

"Blaine. After my horse and a couple of others."

The door opened and Rice stepped out. He glanced sharply at Coker, then over at Timm. "All right. Better ride your horses back up the canyon. There's an old corral there where they won't be seen. I'll come along."

At the brush corral, he watched them strip the saddles from their tired horses and saddle up afresh. Utah got his kak on the lineback and the stallion nudged him happily with its nose. "You haven't seen us," he explained to Rice.

Rice chuckled wryly. "I wasn't born yesterday. You boys watch your step."

He backed up, holding the gate open for them. As they passed he looked up at Timm. "I s'pose you know you're ridin' with a couple of wolves?"

Timm chuckled. "Sure do," he said cheerfully, "an' you know, Rice, I feel fifteen years younger! Anyway," he added, "I like the company of wolves better than coyotes." ·

Four days later, worn and hollow-eyed, they rested in Calfpen Canyon. Hunkered over a fire they watched the coffee water come to a boil. Then Timm dumped in the grounds. There was a bloody bandage on Coker's head and all of them were honed down and fine with hunger and hard riding. The horses showed it even more than the men.

"Ridin' with the wolves is rough, Timm," Blaine said.

The older man looked up. The grizzled beard on his jaws made him seem even older than he was. "I like it, Utah." His voice was low. "Only one thing I want. I want to fight back."

"That," Blaine said quietly, "starts the day after tomorrow. We're goin' to swing wide to the east an', take our time, let our horses rest up from the hard goin' and swing away around to the Big N."

Rip Coker looked up. His hatchet face was even thinner now, his tight, hard mouth like a gash.

"We're goin' to hit back," Utah said, "an' hard. We're goin' to show 'em what war means!"

"Now you're talkin'!" Rip's voice was harsh with emotion. "I'm fed up with runnin'!"

"They haven't seen us for a day now," Utah said, "and they'll not see us again for a couple more. We'll let 'em relax while we rest up."

Nevers was dead tired. He stripped off his clothes and crawled gratefully into the blankets. In the adjoining room he heard the hands slowly turning in. There was little talk among them tonight, and he stared gloomily at his boots. The chase, which had started off with excitement, was growing dull for them, and when not dull, dangerous.

On the second day they had caught up with Blaine and his two companions and in the gun battle that followed two of the Big N riders had been wounded, one of them seriously. One of the Blaine group had gone down—Coker, somebody had said. But they had escaped and carried the wounded man with them.

Twice the following day Nevers and his men lost the trail, and then, at daybreak of the next day, it vanished completely. After several hours of futile search they had given up and wearily rode back to the Big N.

Nevers stretched out and drew the blankets over him. There was still the matter of Fox. The Table Mountain rancher had moved into the house on the 46 and had a rider on the B-Bar. The Big N also had a rider there, and it was believed Ben Otten was to send a man to establish his claim also.

Nevers awakened with a start. How long he had been asleep he did not know, but some sound outside the house had awkened him. Rising to an elbow, he listened intently. He heard the snort of a horse, the crack of a rope on a flank, and then the thunder of hoofs. Somebody was after the horses!

He swung his feet to the floor and grabbed for his boots. In the adjoining room a match flared and a light was lit. Then a shot smashed the lamp chimney to bits and he heard the crack of the shot mingling with the tinkle of falling glass.

With a grunt of fury, Nevers sprang for his rifle, but a bullet smashed the window frame and thudded into the wall within inches of his rifle stock. Other bullets shattered other windows. A shot struck the pot-bellied stove in the next room and rico-cheted about, and somebody yelled with sudden pain. Outside there was a wild yell, and more shots. Nevers grabbed his rifle and got to the window. A shot scattered wood fragments in his eyes and he dropped his rifle and clawed at his face, swearing bitterly.

More shots sounded, and then there was a sudden glare of light from outside. Through his tear-filled eyes, Nevers blinked at the glare. His carefully gathered hay stack was going up in flames!

With a roar, he grabbed up his rifle and rushed from the house. Somewhere he heard a yell. "You wanted war, Nevers! How do you like it?" A shot spat dirt over his bare feet, and more glass sprinkled behind him.

Impotent with fury, he fired off into the dark and then rushed toward the barn. The others joined him and for more than an hour they fought desperately to save the barn. The hay was a total loss: ten tons of it gone up in smoke!

Wearily, sodden with fatigue, they trooped back to the house where coffee was being made. "I'll kill him!" Nevers blared. "I'll see him hung!"

Nobody said anything. They sat down, sagging with exhaustion. After the hard ride of the past few days the fight against the fire had done them in, all of them. And they still had to round up their horses.

Only one man had been hurt. Flying glass had cut his face, producing a very slight, but painful cut.

The man wounded in the gunfight during the chase raised up in bed. "That Blaine," he called out, "ain't no bargain!"

"Shut up!" Nevers turned on him. "Shut your mouth!"

All was quiet in the house. Finally, Rocky White got up and stretched. "I reckon," he said slowly, "I'll go to sleep outside." He walked out. Then slowly a couple of the hands got up and followed him.

Nevers stared after them, his face sour. Viciously, he swore. That damned Blaine!

The other hands drifted one by one back to sleep, and then the light winked out. The sky was already gray in the east. Nevers slumped on the bed, staring at the gray rectangle of the window. The bitterness within him was turning to a deep and vindictive hatred of Blaine. Heretofore the gunfighter had merely represented an obstacle to be overcome. Now he represented something more.

There was only one answer. He would get Rink Witter to round up a few paid killers and he would start them out, professional man-hunters. Fox would chip in, maybe Otten, too. They could pay five or six men a good price to hunt Blaine, and get up a bounty on his scalp.

Wearily he got to his feet and walked outside. He saddled up and swung into the saddle. One of the hands stuck his head out of the barn. Nevers shouted back, "I'll be back tomorrow! Ridin' to Red Creek!"

Mary Blake had arrived in Red Creek only a short time before the night attack on the Big N. Restive, unable to await results in the Mormon community, she had boarded the stage for Red Creek with Maria. The next morning the first person she met was Ralston Forbes.

"Hello!" He looked at her with surprise. "I heard you left the country."

"I've not gone and I've no intention of going. Have you seen Utah?"

"No, but I've heard plenty. Nevers has been hot on his trail. They had a scrap the other night with honors about even by all accounts. What are you planning to do?"

She smiled at him. "Have breakfast and not tell any plans to a newspaperman."

"Come on, then! We'll have breakfast together." They walked across the street to the cafe just in time to meet Otten at the door. He stared at her gloomily, then looked at Forbes.

"Any news?" he asked.

"Not a word."

They opened the door and stepped into the cafe and stopped abruptly. Blaine, Timm and Rip Coker were seated at the table eating. All were unshaven, dirty and obviously close to exhaustion. Utah looked up, his eyes going from one to the other. They hesitated on Mary, then went on to Otten. He said nothing at all.

"You're taking a chance," Forbes suggested.

"We're used to it," Blaine replied. "Has Ortmann been around?"

"No. He isn't showing his face since you whipped him. What do you want with him?"

"Suppose I'd tell you with one of the enemy in camp?" Blaine asked.

Otten flushed and started to speak, but Rip Coker interrupted him. "Straddlin' a rail can give a man a mighty sore crotch, Ben."

The banker looked from one to the other, his face sour. "Can't a man even eat his breakfast in peace?" he complained.

Utah looked at Mary. "You came back. Why?"

"I couldn't—just couldn't let you do it alone. I wanted to help."

Nobody said anything for several minutes. Utah ate tiredly, and the girl came in and filled his coffee cup. The hot black coffee tasted good, very good.

Rip's bandage was fresh. They had awakened the doctor for that, and he had bandaged the scalp wound after making some ironic comments about hard heads.

"Anything for publication?" Forbes asked, finally.

Blaine looked up. His eyes were bloodshot. "Why, sure," he grinned suddenly, "say that Utah Blaine, manager of the 46 Connected, is vacationing in the hills for a few days but expects to be back at Headquarters soon. You might add that he expects to return to attend the funerals of several of the leading citizens of the valley—and he hopes their respected banker, Ben Otten, will not be one of them."

Otten looked up, his face flushing. Before he could open his mouth, however, there was a clatter of horse's hoofs and then boots struck the boardwalk and the door burst open.

In the open door, her face flushed from riding in the wind, her dark eyes bright with excitement, was Angie Kinyon!

"Utah! You've got to ride!" She was breathless with hurry. "Lee Fox struck your trail and he's coming right on with a pack of men. Nevers joined him outside of town! Hurry, please!"

Blaine got to his feet, hitching his gun belts. He looked across the table at Angie and his eyes softened. "Thanks," he said. "Thanks very much!"

Mary Blake looked startled. Her eyes went quickly from one to the other. Ralston Forbes was watching her and he was smiling.

CHAPTER XI

WHEN THEY were gone Mary Blake looked over at Angie. "It's a surprise to see you here, Angie," she said graciously, but with just the slightest edge to her voice. "You don't often ride to town. Especially at this hour."

Angie smiled gaily, but her mind was not in the room. It was out there on the trail with the galloping horses. Forbes could see it, and so could Mary. "No," Angie said, "I don't often come in, but when a friend is in danger, that changes everything."

"I didn't know you even knew Utah Blaine," Mary said too casually.

"We only met once."

"Once?" Mary was ironic. Her chin lifted slightly. Ralston Forbes grinned. He was seeing Mary Blake jealous for the first time and it amused him.

Angie was suddenly aware. She smiled beautifully. "Isn't once enough?"

"I suppose it is," Mary replied stiffly, "but if I were you, Angie, I'd be careful. You know how these drifting punchers are."

"No." Angie's voice was deadly sweet. "You tell me. How are they, Mary?"

Mary Blake's face went white and she started from her chair. "What do you mean by that?" she flared. "What are you trying to insinuate?"

Angie's surprise was eloquent. "Why nothing! Nothing at all, Mary! Only you seemed so worried about me, and your advice sounded so—so experienced."

Mary Blake turned abruptly to Forbes, but before she could speak there was a clatter of horses' hoofs. A dozen riders swung to a halt before the door. It smashed open and Lee Fox stepped in. "Where are they? Where's Blaine?"

Angie turned slowly and looked at him, her eyes cool. She said nothing at all. Mary shrugged and walked to the window and Lee's face flamed with anger. He stepped into the room and strode toward Angie. "You!" he shouted, his face contorted. "You just rode in! I seen your horse out here, all lathered! You warned him!"

"And what if I did?" Her eyes blazed. "I should stay here and let an honest man be murdered by a pack of renegade land thieves?"

Lee Fox gasped. His anger rendered him speechless. "Thieves?" He all but screamed the word. "You call us thieves? What about that—that—"

"I call you thieves." Angie said it quietly. "Lee Fox, neither you nor anyone else has one particle of claim to that land, nor to the B-Bar. Both ranches were used by far better men who got here first. You've been snarling like a pack of coyotes around a grizzly for years. Now the bear is dead and you rush in like the carrion hunting scavengers you are, to grab off the ranches they built! You have no vestige of claim on either place except your greed. If anyone has a just claim on the 46 it is Utah Blaine."

"Utah?" Fox was wild, incredulous. "What claim would he have?"

"He was left in charge. That is claim enough. At least," she shrugged, "it is more claim than you have." Her tone changed. "Why don't you be sensible, Lee? Go back to your ranch and be satisfied with what you have while there's still a chance? You don't know what you're doing."

Fox stepped toward her, his eyes glittering. "You —you—" His hand lifted.

"Fox!" Forbes barked the name, and Lee froze, shocked into realization. His eyes swung and stopped. Ralston Forbes held a six-shooter in his hand. "You make another move toward that girl and I'll kill you!"

Fox lowered his hand slowly, controlling himself with an effort. "You keep out of this," he said thickly.

"Fox, you've evidently forgotten how people think of Angie Kinyon in this country. If you struck her your own men would hang you. You'd not live an hour."

"I wasn't goin' to hit her." Fox controlled himself, pressing his lips together. "She ain't got no right to talk that way."

"When your common sense overcomes your greed, Fox, you'll see that every word she said was truth. Furthermore," Forbes said quietly, "I intend to print just that in my paper tomorrow!"

Fox's eyes were ugly. "You do an' I'll smash that printin' press an' burn you out! You been carryin' it high an' mighty long enough. There's a new system comin' into bein' around here. If you don't think like we do, we'll either change you or kill you!"

Forbes was tall. He looked taller now. "That's your privilege to try, Fox. But I wouldn't if I were you. There are some things this country won't tolerate. Abuse of a good woman and interference with a free press are two of them."

Fox stared at Mary Blake. He started to speak, then turned abruptly and strode from the room. Then there was a rattle of horses' hoofs and they were gone.

"Thanks, Rals," Angie said. "He would have hit me."

Forbes nodded. "And I'd have killed him. And I've never killed a man, Angie."

"At least," Angie said, "Blaine will have more of a start. They'll not catch him now."

"No."

Mary Blake turned from the window. "What about you, Rals? You'd better not try to fight them. You're all alone here."

"Alone?" Forbes shook his head. "No, I'm not alone. There's a dozen men here in town who'll stand by me: Ryan, the blacksmith, Jordan, the shoemaker, all of them."

It was only an hour later that news reached Red Creek of the attack on the Big N. Ben Otten was in the cafe talking to Forbes when a Big N hand came in. They listened to Rocky White's recital of what had happened. Ten tons of hay gone! Although worth twenty-five dollars a ton now, the hay would be priceless before the coming winter was gone.

And the ranch house had been shot up. More and more he was beginning to realize that once trouble was started anything could happen. He tried his coffee and stared glumly out the window.

Rocky White said nothing for a few minutes. Then he commented, "The Old Man's fit to be tied. He's sure cuttin' capers over this shootin'. I wonder what he figured would happen when he braced Utah Blaine? Lucky the man isn't an out an' out killer. He'd have killed Nevers by now."

"What's Nevers goin' to do?" Otten asked.

"He's importin' gunmen. He's goin' to hunt Blaine down an' kill him. He's sent Witter after some gun-

94

slingers. He's goin' to offer a flat thousand for Blaine's scalp, five hundred for the other two. Five hundred each, that is."

"That will blow the lid off. We'll have a United States Marshal in here."

The cowhand got up. "Yeah, an' a good thing, too," he said. "Well, so long." He glanced around. "I'm draggin' my freight. I want no part of it,"

The leave-taking of Rocky White created a restlessness among the other hands. Two of Otten's oldest cowhands suddenly pulled out without even talking to him, leaving wages behind. A man quit Fox the same way. In the meanwhile, however, men came in to replace them, five of them were gunfighters.

Now the chase was growing intense. One by one the waterholes were being located and men were staked out near them. Blaine found that Rice's cabin was no longer safe. It was being watched. Even the corral back in the brush had been located and was under constant observation. Blaine struck Fox's Table Mountain outfit at midnight on the third day after the Big N raid. Only two men were at home. They were tied up, the horses were turned loose and driven off, the water trough ripped out and turned over, the corral burned.

Clell Miller and Timm exchanged shots but both missed. Rip Coker came upon one, Pete Scantlin, an Indian tracker working for Nevers' man-hunters. The Indian had his eyes on the ground. He looked up suddenly and saw Rip sitting his horse, and the Indian threw up his rifle. His shot went wild when Rip's .44 ripped through his throat. The body was found an hour later. Written in the dust alongside the body were the words:

NO QUARTER FOR MAN-HUNTERS. YOU ASK FOR IT, YOU GET IT.

Soon after two of Nevers' gunhands shot up Red Creek while on a drunken spree, wounding one bystander with flying glass. Forbes' paper came out on schedule with a headline that shouted to the world and all who would read:

LAWLESSNESS RAMPANT IN VALLEY. ATTEMPTED LAND GRAB BY NEVERS, FOX AND OTTEN LEADS TO KILLINGS

That night men with sledge hammers broke into his printing office and smashed one of his presses. Forbes' arrival with a smoking gun drove them off. His ire fully roused now, the following morning Forbes mailed copies of the paper, of which only a few had been left unburned, to the governor of the territory, to the United States Marshal and to newspapers in El Paso, Santa Fe and other western towns.

However, following the Fox raid no word came from Blaine. The rumor spread that he was wounded. The death of Scantlin was attributed to Blaine until Rip Coker drifted into town.

He came riding in just before closing time at the Verde Saloon. He pushed through the doors and walked to the bar. His face was drawn, his eyes sparking and grim. He tossed off a drink and turned to face the half-dozen men in the room. "Folks say Utah killed Pete Scantlin. It wasn't Utah. It was me. Utah can stand for his own killin's, I stand for mine. He was huntin' me down like a varmint, so I rode out an' gave him his chance. He lost."

"You better ride, Rip. Clell's huntin' you."

"Huntin' me? Where is he?"

"In his room over at the hotel," somebody said. "But you . . . you better—" The speaker's voice broke sharply off for Clell Miller stood in the doorway.

Miller's face had sharpened and hardened. His eyes were ugly and it was obvious that he had been drinking—not enough to make him unsteady, but more than enough to arouse all his latent viciousness.

"Huntin' me, Rip?" Clell stepped in and let the door close behind him. "I saw you ride in. Thought I'd come down."

"Sure, I'm huntin' you." Rip Coker stepped away from the bar. His thin, hard-boned face was drawn and fine from the hard riding and short rations, but his smile was reckless and eager. "You want it now?"

"Why not?" Clell went for his gun as he spoke and it came up, incredibly fast, faster than that of Rip Coker. His first shot struck Rip right over the belt buckle and Rip took an involuntary step back. Clell fired again and missed, but Rip steadied his hand before he fired. His shot spun Miller around. Miller dropped to one knee and fired from the floor. His second shot hit Rip, and then Rip brought his gun down and shot twice, both bullets hitting Clell in the head. Clell fell over, slammed back by the force of the bullets.

Rip staggered, his face pale. He started, staggering for the door. As he stepped out, a voice from across the street called out. "We get five hundred for you Rip!" And then a half-dozen guns went off. Slammed back into the wall by the force of the bullets, Rip brought up his own gun. His knees wavered, but he stiffened them. He was mortally wounded, but he straightened his knees and fired. A man staggered and went down, and Rip fired again. Bullets struck him, but he kept feeding shells into his gun.

Shot to doll rags, he would not go down. He fired again and then again. Somebody up the street yelled and then another ragged volley crashed into the blond fighter. He fired again as he fell, and one of the killers rose on his toes and fell headlong.

Forbes rushed from the hotel, Mary Blake and Angie following him. Ben Otten and others began to crowd around. Rink Witter pushed through the crowd. "Back off," he snarled. "If this varmint ain't dead, he soon will be!"

Forbes looked at him, his face drawn in hard lines in the light from the Verde window. "Leave him alone, you murderer!" he said. "You've done enough!"

Rink Witter's eyes glittered and he looked down. The doctor had come up and was kneeling over Coker. Coker's eyes fluttered and he looked up at Witter. Suddenly, the dying man chuckled. "Wait! Wait!" he whispered hoarsely. "You're dead, Rink! Wait'll Blaine hears of this! He'll hang up your scalp!"

"Shut up!" Witter snarled.

Rip grinned weakly. "Not—not bad," he whispered, "I got Clell. Nev—figured—I'd—I'd beat him."

The bartender, an admirer of gameness in any man, leaned over. "You can go happy, son," he said. "You got two more to take along."

Rip put a feeble hand on the doctor's arm. "You —wastin' time, sawbones." He blinked slowly. "Clell an' two more! Hell, I don't reckon Utah could of done much better!"

The doctor straightened slowly and looked over at Forbes. "I can't understand it," he whispered. "He's shot to ribbons. He should be dead."

Angie moved in. "Carry him to my room, Doc. He's got nerve enough for two men. Maybe he'll come through."

By mid-morning the story was all over the valley. Rip Coker had shot it out with Clell Miller and killed him. Staggering from the saloon, badly wounded, he had been ambushed by six gunmen, had killed two of them before going down under a hail of bullets. Although shot eleven times, he was still alive!

"He might make it," Forbes told Angie. "Cole Younger was shot eleven times in the fighting during and after the Northfield raid, and he lived."

"Yeah," the bartender was listening. "I was tendin' bar in Coffeyville when the Daltons raided it. Emmett was shot *sixteen* times in that raid. Hear he's still alive."

Utah Blaine had been scouting the 46 range. When he returned to their temporary hideout in the Gorge near Whiterock Mesa, Timm came down to him, his face dark with worry. "See anything of Rip?" he asked. "He took off when I was asleep last night. Never said a word."

Blaine swung down. His jaws were dark with four days' growth of beard, his eyes hollow from lack of sleep. "That damn' fool!" he said anxiously. "He's gone huntin' a fight! Saddle up an' we'll ride in!"

"No," Timm said, "you get some rest. If Rip is still

alive now, he'll stay alive. You go down there like you are and you'll be duck soup for whoever runs into you first. Get some sleep."

It was wise advice and Blaine knew it. In a matter of minutes he was asleep. Timm looked down at his face and shook his head. Slowly, he walked out in the sunlight and sat among the rocks where he could watch both approaches to the Gorge. There was small chance of their being found here, but it could happen. He was tired himself, when he thought about it. Very tired.

Far down on the river bank, an Apache signaled to Rink, motioning him over. "One horse," the Indian said. "He ver' tired—cross here."

"A big horse?" Witter asked eagerly.

"Uh-huh, ver' big."

Blaine's dun stallion, the lineback stallion, was larger than most of the horses around here. Rink Witter rubbed his jaw thoughtfully and squinted his glittering little eyes as he studied the terrain before him. The great triangular bow of the mesa jutted against the skyline some three miles away. It was all of fifteen hundred feet above them, and the country to both left and right was broken and rugged. A man on a tired horse would not go far, and a man who was exhausted, as Utah Blaine must be, would have to bed down somewhere. Nor would he be watching the covering of his trail so carefully.

"Let's shake down those canyons left of the mesa," he said, "I've got a hunch.

Slightly less than six miles away, Timm sat in the warm sunshine. He was very tired. The warmth seeped through his weary muscles, easing them and relaxing them. Below him a rattler crawled into the shade and a deer walked down to a pool of water and drank. Timm shifted his seat a little, but did not open his eyes.

It felt mighty good to be resting. Mighty good. And it was warm after the chill of the night. His eyelids flicked open, then lowered . . . closed . . . they started to open . . . then closed again. Timm was not as young as Rip or Blaine. This riding took its toll. Slowly, his eyes closed tighter and he slept.

CHAPTER XII

THE MOUNTAINS into which Rink Witter led his four men were rugged and heavily wooded. Skirting the lower shoulder of a mesa, he headed across an open stretch of exposed Coconino sandstone and swung back toward the river.

Ceaselessly he searched out the possible hideouts that could be used by two exhausted men and their worn mounts. North of the towering wall of the mesa there were a half-dozen deep canyons. Each of these canyons had occasional seeps from intermittent streams where a man might obtain water.

Even without a cache of food there was game back here: deer, elk, bear and plenty of birds. A man could scarcely ask for a better hideout. Rink was in no hurry. Hunched atop his horse, he studied the terrain with his flat-lidded eyes. Trust Blaine to pick a hole with a back way out. Yet if they took their time, Blaine might relax. He was tired. He had to be tired. And after a few minutes he would relax and sink down, and possibly he would go to sleep.

Wardlaw, one of Rink's special men, studied the terrain with care. "Country for an ambush," he commented. "This Blaine ain't no tenderfoot."

It was nearing sundown before they completed an examination of the two canyons to their north and started up the main canyon called the Gorge, which led almost due east. They had gone scarcely a half mile when the tracker lifted a hand. Plain enough for all to see were the marks of a horse crossing a stream.

All drew up. Wardlaw struck a match and squinted past the smoke at Rink. "Figure it's far?"

Rink looked speculatively up the Gorge. "This canyon," he told them, "takes a sharp turn about two miles east. My guess would be they'll be located right up there at the foot of Whiterock Mesa. There's an undercut wall there, plenty of firewood an' good water.

"I say," he continued, "that we take her mighty easy. If we come along quiet we may come right up on them."

Timm came awake with a start, horrified at what he had done. Hours must have passed for it was already past sundown. He started to move, and then he stopped. Not sixty yards away were Rink Witter and his killers!

They saw him at the same instant. Wardlaw's gun leaped and blazed. The shot sprinkled rock on Timm, and he swung his rifle. His own quick shot would have taken Rink but for the fact that the gelding Rink rode chose that instant to swing his head and the shot took him between the eyes. The horse went down, creating momentary confusion, but Wardlaw fired again, knocking Timm back into the rocks. Rolling over, he started to crawl.

Utah came out of his sound sleep wide awake. He sprang to his feet and threw himself into the shelter of a rock before he realized the shooting was centering about a hundred yards away. Hastily he swung saddles on the two horses and cinched them. Then he threw the packs on. It was the work of a minute for all had been kept ready for instant travel.

He heard another shot behind him and knew that for the moment Timm was doing all right. But Blaine also knew they couldn't hold this spot longer than a few minutes. However, it was, fortunately, close to night. He left the horses standing and raced down the short canyon to the main branch. The first thing he saw was Timm. The older man was crouched by some boulders, his rifle ready, his back stained with blood. That the man was hard hit, Utah saw at once.

Sliding up beside him, he whispered, "Stay in there, partner!"

Timm's face was agonized. "I went to sleep!" he was shocked with the shame of it.

Blaine grinned. "Hell, you couldn't have seen 'em until they were right on you, anyway!" The Apache showed and Blaine burned him with a shot across the shoulder, then slammed a fast shot at a shelving rock that ricocheted the bullet into the shelter taken by the killers. Lead smashed around him.

He glanced at Timm. Hard hit he was, but he was still able to move. "Start crawlin'," he said. "I took time to saddle the horses. Get to 'em, an' if you can, get into the saddle."

Utah shifted left and fired, then shifted back halfway to his original position and fired again. A shrewd and experienced Indian fighter, he knew just exactly what their chances were. The men against them were bloodhounds, and fighting men, too. They would be on the trail and fast, and they were men one couldn't gamble with.

Suddenly, a shot clipped rock near him, and he

noticed where it came from. Right up from behind a boulder on a steep slope. The boulder was propped by a small rock while behind it was piled a heap of debris. Snuggling his rifle against his shoulder, he took careful aim at the rock, then fired!

The rock splintered and the boulder sagged. Carefully, Blaine took another sight, and then fired again. He never knew whether it was the first shot or the second that started it, but just as his finger squeezed off that second shot the whole pile tore loose and thundered down the hill!

There was a startled yell, then another. Two men sprang into the open and with calm dispatch, Utah Blaine drilled the first through the chest, and dropped the second with a bullet that appeared to have struck his knee. The rocks roared down, swung sharply as they struck a shoulder of rock, then poured down into the stream bed.

Swiftly, before the man-hunters would have time to adjust themselves, Utah turned and raced back up the canyon to the horses. Timm was in the saddle, slumped over the pommel. His rifle was on the ground. Picking it up, Utah dropped it in the bucket and they started. He led Timm's horse and went right straight for a dim mountain trail between huge boulders. Beyond it there was brush. The shadows were heavy now and it would soon be dark. With an occasional glance back at the wounded man, he rode swiftly.

Now they climbed through the pines, mounting swiftly on a winding, switch-back trail. Darkness filled the bowl of the valley below and the dark gash of the canyon; it bulked thick and black under the tall pines. Beyond them, far to the south, the sunlight lay a golden glory on the four peaks of the Mazatzals.

With a mile more of the winding mountain trail behind him, he turned into the pine forest and crossed the thick cushioned needles and then took a trail that dipped down into the basin of Rock Creek. Instead of following it south toward their cached food and ammunition, Utah turned left and went up the canyon of Rock Creek itself. Then he crossed a saddle to another creek.

Glancing back, seeing that Timm was still in the saddle, he grimly pushed on. Hours later, and then he sighted his objective: a canyon crossed by a natural bridge of rock. Dipping deep into this canyon he worked his way along it until he reached the caves of which, long since, he had heard described.

When he stopped Timm swayed and Utah reached up and lifted the older man from the saddle. Timm's face was pale, visible even in the vague light near the cave's mouth. "I stuck it, didn't I?" he whispered, then fainted.

There was a sand floor in one of the caves, and Blaine led the horses there. He drew them well back from the entrance and out of sight; then he built a fire. No one could ever find them here.

When water was hot he uncovered Timm's wounds and bathed them carefully. The older man was hard hit, and how he had stayed so long in the saddle was nothing short of a miracle. Carefully, he bandaged the wounds and then sat beside the old man and prepared food.

Outside, the air was damp and there was a hint of coming rain. He listened to the far-off rumble of thunder and was thankful for the shelter of the cave. The rain, if it came, would wipe out their tracks.

On the adverse side, they were far from their

caches of food and Timm was in no shape to be moved. Moreover, wherever he was, Rip Coker might be needing them. Timm stirred and muttered, and then moaned softly. He looked bad, but there was no medicine . . . suddenly from the dark archives of memory came a thought . . . something he had not remembered in years.

Going to the sack of maize carried for horse feed, he took out several cups' full. Making a grinding stone of a flat rock, he crushed the maize to meal and then made a mush which he bound on the wound. This was, he recalled, an Indian remedy that he had seen used long ago. Then he made a like poultice for the other wound. When next he walked to the cave entrance he saw the rain pouring down past the opening. Luckily, the entrance of the cave was high enough so that water could not come into the cave mouth.

The horses pricked their ears at him and he curried them both, taking time out to walk back to his patient. Finally Timm awakened. Supporting him with a raised knee, Utah fed him slowly from a thick hot soup he had made from maize and jerky. Timm was conscious but had no knowledge of where he was.

When finally the old-timer dozed off again, Utah walked to the cave mouth. The stream had risen and was washing down the canyon bottom deep enough to wipe out any tracks made there, and probably it would erase the tracks left on the high ground as well. Seeing driftwood just beyond the cave mouth, Utah gathered some of it and dragged it inside where it would have a chance to dry. Then he returned to his patient and changed the maize poultice on the wounds. Then adding fuel to the fire so that it would continue to give off a low flame, he rolled up in his own blankets and slept.

Blaine prepared some breakfast and used the last of the maize for a new poultice. Timm seemed a little better. He ate some of the grub, and seemed in improved spirits.

"Not bad," he said, grinning. "My old lady couldn't've done better."

"Didn't know you were married, Timm."

"I'm not no more. Amy died . . . cholera."

"Too bad."

Timm said nothing and Utah Blaine got to his feet. "Will you be all right? I want to hunt some herbs that may help those wounds."

"Go ahead."

Blaine started for the door and then looked back. Timm was staring after him. "Utah," his voice shook a little, "you—you—think we'll ever get back? You think—" His voice trailed weakly off.

"We'll get back, Timm," Blaine promised, "you'll be back on the old job again."

"Reckon I'd rather work for you," Timm said quietly. "I reckon I would."

It was an hour before Utah returned. In his arms he had a stack of herbs used by the Indians to doctor wounds and—he stopped. "Timm?"

There was no reply. Blaine dropped his load and rushed forward. He needed only a glance.

Timm was dead. He had died quietly, smiling a little.

Utah Blaine looked down at him. "I'd like to have had you work with me. You were a good man, Timm. A mighty good man."

Wearily, he gathered up the guns and ammunition. And now he was alone . . . Alone. And somewhere out there they were hunting him. Hunting him like a wild animal.

CHAPTER XIII

DESPITE her worry over Utah Blaine, Angie had not returned to her small home. So she was standing in the hotel with Rals Forbes when they saw Rink Witter come in. Two men rode with him, and two more were across their saddles. One of the riding men was wounded. Her face stiff, Angie looked down upon the little cavalcade.

Forbes turned abruptly. "I'm going down there. I'm going to find out what happened."

Angie followed him, walking quickly. Slowly, the street began to fill. Nevers was in town this morning as was Lee Fox. Lud Fuller was also there, his face somber. Fuller never talked these days.

Ben Otten came down the street and stopped beside Nevers. He looked up at Rink, feeling the cruelty in that dark, leather-like face. "No," Witter said, "we didn't get Blaine. He got away an' took Timm with him, but I think Timm was bad hurt. We trailed 'em over Whiterock Mesa but lost 'em near Rock Creek. He was headed south toward the Mazatzals, but he couldn't have gone that far, not with Timm hurt an' his horses tired."

"You lost some men."

Rink Witter turned to Forbes, who made the statement. "Huntin' Blaine ain't no picnic," he said harshly. "They killed two men for me an' one horse. An' Wardlaw's wounded."

Rink swung to the ground. "Utah's an Injun on the trail," he said flatly, stating a fact. "He don't leave no more trail 'n wolf."

108

"You think you got Timm?" It was Fox who asked the question.

Witter nodded. "Figure so."

"Then Blaine's alone," Nevers said, "he'll quit."

Lud Fuller stirred. "He won't quit. I seen him fight Ortmann. He don't know what the word means."

Nevers glared at Fuller. Then he turned and moved toward the hotel. "Come in, Rink. We'll make talk."

Forbes turned and looked at Angie. "What can we do?" he said. "It's plain hell to want to do something and have your hands tied. My press is coming around, but I doubt if I'll get more than one paper off before they bust it up again."

"I wish the governor would write."

"He probably threw the paper away."

Mary Blake came down the street, switching her leg with a quirt. She stopped, looking from one to the other. "He's out there," she said. "I'm going looking for him."

"You'd better leave him alone," Angie replied shortly. "That's all he'd need would be a woman leading Rink Witter to him."

"I'll find him. And Rink Witter won't trail me, either. I can lose him."

"Coker and now Timm. He's all alone out there."

"It's not your fight," Mary said quietly. "There's no reason for you to worry."

Angie made no reply, turning slightly to look at Forbes. She looked down the street. A tall man in black was walking up from the station. He carried a carpetbag in his right hand. He paused, then came on over to where they stood. He was a gray-haired man with sharp, quick eyes.

"How do you do?" he said. "I am George Padjen, attorney-at-law. May I ask to whom I am speaking?"

"I'm Ralston Forbes." Forbes eyes smiled. "I was the local editor until my press was smashed up." Suddenly his interest quickened. "You're not from the governor?"

"No," the man smiled, "I'm not. I was told that I should be very careful about who I talked to, but your name was on the favorable list."

"May I introduce Miss Kinyon? And Miss Blake?"

Padjen removed his hat with a flourish, then looked at Forbes. "Where's Utah Blaine? Is he on the 46?"

Briefly, Forbes outlined the events of the past few days: the fight with Ortmann, the attack on Blaine at the ranch, the escape and the killing of Kelsey and then of Coker and the probable killing of Timm.

"But you said Coker was still alive?" Padjen objected.

Forbes smiled wryly. "As a matter of fact, he is. However, the man hasn't a chance. The doctor has been expecting him to die ever since he was shot. Somehow he has hung on. But as far as Utah goes, Coker might as well be dead. He's out of the running."

"My news seems to be important then," Padjen said quietly. "Before Joe Neal returned here he came to me and made a will. If anything happened to him the ranch was to go to Blaine."

"*What?*" Forbes' shout turned heads. "You're telling the truth?"

"I am."

Forbes grabbed his arm. "Come on then!" Quickly he rushed him down to the newspaper office. "This," he said, "I'll set up and run off by hand!"

With both girls helping and Padjen explaining further details, Rals Forbes stripped off his coat and went to work. Quickly, he ran off twenty handbills. They carried the story in short, concise sentences following a scarehead in heavy black type.

! ! ! JOE NEAL WILLS 46 TO BLAINE ! ! !

According to a will filed for probate in El Paso, Joe Neal willed the 46 Connected with all cattle, horses and appurtenances thereto to Utah Blaine, to take effect immediately upon his death. THIS DEFINITELY THROWS OUT ANY CLAIMS TO THIS RANGE ADVANCED BY THE ASSOCIATED RANCHERS WHO HAVE ATTACKED AND KILLED HANDS FROM THE 46 AND B-BAR RANCHES.

According to the terms of the will Blaine may never sell, lease, or yield up any rights or privileges of the 46 to any of the ranchers now in the valley. THE LAST SHADOW OF A CLAIM MADE BY THESE RANCHERS IS NOW REMOVED AND IF THEY PERSIST IN THESE MURDEROUS ATTACKS THEY WILL BE OUTLAWS AND MUST BE TREATED AS SUCH!

Padjen grinned and looked up at Forbes. "If you tack these up you'd better barricade yourself or leave town!"

Forbes nodded ruefully. "I've been thinking of that, believe me, I have!" Then he looked up at them and picked up some handbills. "Hell, I asked for it," he said, "here goes!"

Padjen's eyes twinkled. He shifted his gun to the

front and picked up a few of the remaining handbills and walked out.

Angie moved slowly from the building and stood on the street. She knew now what would happen. Or she believed she did. For what else could happen? Nevers had gone too far to back up now. So had Fox. They had killed men, killed them unjustly; killed them in a wild grab for range. Now the last vestige of right had been taken from them. They had no shadow of legality to their claims, yet had they ever had such a right where the B-Bar was concerned? And now the 46 Connected was definitely Blaine's.

Somewhere out there in the hills Utah was wandering now, perhaps wounded, certainly hungry. Could Mary Blake reach him without leading Witter to Blaine? No, not even if she knew right where to go. She was not skillful enough. But this was not true of Angie. She did know . . . she turned abruptly and walked swiftly down the street.

Far back in the hills near the caves, Utah Blaine finished his burial of Timm. Over the grave he said a few simple words, and then he gathered a few flowers and planted them near the crude cross he had made.

He stepped back and looked at the grave. "See you, Timm!" He turned and walked to his horse. Mounting, with Timm's horse behind him, he started southwest down Pine Canyon. For the first time in his life he was going on the hunt. He was going to seek out three men and kill them.

Blaine rode swiftly. When he had covered five miles, he shifted horses and rode Timm's gelding. In this manner he pushed on through the night, holding his gait steady, and averaging a good eight to ten miles an hour over all kinds of country. At daybreak he released Timm's horse, retaining only the old-timer's guns. He now had two rifles, a shotgun and three pistols—all loaded.

Yet he needed food. It had been days since he had enjoyed a decent meal and Angie's cabin was only a few miles north. He turned the lineback north along the river trail. Not more than an hour after daybreak he rode up to the cabin. The first thing he saw was the thin trail of smoke from the kitchen chimney. The second was the saddled horse standing at the corral gate.

Riding his own horse into the pines behind the cabin, he tied it there and then, with the shotgun in his hands, he worked his way forward under the trees. When he reached the big sycamore under which he and Angie had talked, he paused and made a careful survey of all the ground in sight. He found no tracks but those of the girl and her horse. Warily, he looked over the terrain beyond the river. Only then did he walk up to the door. He opened it and stepped inside.

Angie was dressed for riding and she was working swiftly. Only one plate was on the table.

"Got a couple of more eggs, Angie?"

She turned swiftly, her eyes large with shock. "Utah! Oh, thank God! You're here! You're all right!"

"Don't tell me you were worried?" He looked at her somberly. "Were you leaving?"

"To look for you. Utah, Neal's will has been probated in El Paso. He left the ranch to you. Everything to you."

Utah Blaine stared at her. "To *me*? Are you sure?"

"Yes." Quickly, as she put on more eggs, she explained. She gave him the details of the will as she

113

had them from Padjen; she told him what Forbes had done.

Then, "Utah, where's Timm?"

"I buried him at sundown. He was wounded in the Whiterock fight. Have you seen Coker?"

She told him about Rip Coker's desperate fight in town, his killing of Clell Miller and two other men. "And he's still living. He hasn't been conscious for days, but he's alive. The doctor says it isn't reasonable, that he's shot full of holes, and he gave him up days ago—but he still lives."

"You were coming to tell me about Neal's will?" He studied her over the rim of his coffee cup. "What else?"

"Nothing, except—except— Mary's been worried about you, Utah. She was going to ride out." She hesitated. "Are you in love with her, Utah?"

"With Mary?" He was surprised. Angie's back was turned to him and he could not see her face. "Now whatever gave you an idea like that?"

She put eggs and ham on his plate, then a stack of toast. He ate and forgot everything in the wonderful taste of food. For several minutes he said nothing. When he did look up, he grinned, a little ashamed. "Gosh, I was sure hungry! Say, is there a razor in the house?"

"Dad's razor is here. I've kept a few of his things. His razor, his gun—" She went to get it, and while he shaved, she talked.

She watched the razor scrape the lather and thick whiskers from his jaw. It was a long time since she had seen a man shave. She noted how broad his shoulders were. Hurriedly she got up and walked to the door, looking carefully down the trail, then across the river.

"What will they do, Utah? Will they keep after you?"

He turned and looked at her, holding the razor in his hand. For an instant their eyes met and she looked away quickly, flushing and feeling an unaccountable pounding in her breast.

Her question was forgotten. Slowly, he walked over and stood behind her. "Angie . . ." He took hold of her shoulder with his left hand. "Angie, I think . . ." She turned, her eyes large, dark and frightened. His hand slipped down to her waist and drew her to him, and then he bent and kissed her parted lips. She gave a little muffled gasp and clutched him tightly. Neither of them heard the sound of the approaching horse. It was the step on the porch that startled them apart. As one person they turned toward the door.

Mary Blake stood there, her hat in her hand, her face flushed from the wind. Her eyes went from Utah to Angie and her nostrils widened a little. "Well, Angie," she said with an edge in her tone, "I see you got here first!"

"Why—why, I just came home! I—"

"You'd look better," Mary said, "if you'd wipe the lather off your chin, Angie. Or have you taken to shaving?"

"Oh!" Angie gasped and ran for a mirror.

Utah chuckled suddenly. "Hello, Mary. It's rather a surprise seeing you here."

"So I gathered," Mary said dryly. "And if you don't hurry and get out of here you'll get another surprise. Rink Witter isn't far behind me."

CHAPTER XIV

"RINK IS COMING?"

"Yes, but Nevers will be here first, I think. Rink turned from the trail to do a little scouting. Wardlaw is with him, and Lud Fuller."

"And with Nevers?"

"A half-dozen of his riders."

Utah Blaine turned and picked up his hat. "Both of you stay here. I'll manage all right."

He walked outside and around the house. When he reached the stallion, he untied it and led the horse through the trees to the house. The horse had been cropping grass and now he let him drink, but only a little.

When he saw the dust cloud he swung into the saddle and rode down to the ford of the river. The river here was some twenty yards wide and, at the ford, about stirrup deep. He stopped in a grove of trees leaving his horse back out of range in a sheltered hollow.

He saw the riders swing around the bend of the river and come toward him. He let them come while he sat on a rock and smoked a cigarette. When the riders were three hundred yards off he propped his knee on another boulder and lifted the rifle, getting his elbow well under the barrel. Nestling his cheek against the barrel he aimed at Nevers. His intention was not to kill the man. Yet at the moment he was supremely indifferent. If the horse bobbed at the wrong time—he fired.

His intention had been to clip Nevers' ear, and he had held Nevers under his sights as the distance closed. Nevers jerked and clapped a hand to his head and Blaine heard his cry of anguish and could see the blood streaming down the side of his face.

Instantly, there was a hail of bullets and men scattered. Blaine began to fire. One man was diving for cover and Utah shot him through the legs. His second put Nevers' horse down and Nevers was pinned beneath it. Then Blaine fired again, kicking dirt into Nevers' eyes.

"Want to die, Nevers? You bring other men out to fight your dirty battles! How do you like it?"

He fired again, deliberately missing but putting the shot close. "Get dust in your eyes, Nevers? This'll be better!" Blaine fired again, his bullet striking into the sand square in front of Nevers' face. Sand spat into the rancher's eyes.

Blaine waited an instant, then called out, "The rest of you stay out of this an' you won't get hurt. One of you pull that man in and fix up his leg! Go ahead! I won't shoot!"

A cowhand ran out and picked up the wounded man and started back. Blaine held his fire. He heard Nevers yell from the ground. "Go get him, you fools!! Get after him!"

Utah laughed. "I never saw you come after me, Nevers! Not without plenty of help!" He threw another shot close to Nevers. "I'll kill the first man who shows himself on the bank of this stream!"

He took his time, his eyes roving restlessly to prevent a flanking movement. He had a hunch none of the hands were too anxious to come across the river under fire. After all, Nevers had gunmen to do his killing—men who were getting paid warrior's wages. Anyway, probably few of them disliked to see their boss pinned down and scared—and Nevers was scared.

Without help he could not escape from the dead

horse, and Utah Blaine could kill him any time he wished.

"You had Timm killed," Blaine said conversationally. "You had Coker shot up, an' you've hired murderers to get me. You were one of the lynchers who tried to hang Joe Neal an' by all rights I should shoot you full of holes."

Nevers did not speak. He lay still. Now he was aware that Blaine did not intend to kill him. Frightened as he had at first been, he was remembering that not far behind him were Rink Witter and his killers. They would hear the shooting and would know what to do.

Blaine fired again, and then he faded back into the brush and ran to his stallion. Keeping the lineback to soft sand where he made no noise, he circled swiftly and raced the horse for the river. Crossing it, he headed for the trail to head off Witter. He was coming down the mountain through the trees when suddenly he heard a yell. Not two hundred yards away, fanning across the hillside were a dozen riders! It needed only a glance to tell him that these were Fox and his men.

Snapping a quick shot, Utah wheeled the stallion and plunged down the trail. He was just in time to intercept Witter—but this wasn't the way he had planned it. The surprise was complete. He charged down the mountain and hit the little cavalcade at full speed. They had no chance to turn or avoid him: his stallion was heavier and had the advantage of speed. With his bridle reins around his arm, Blaine grabbed a six-shooter and blasted.

A man screamed and threw up his arms and then Blaine hit him. Horses snorted and there was a wild scramble that was swamped with dust. Through the group the lineback plunged and Blaine had a glimpse of Rink Witter's contorted face as the gunman clawed for a pistol. Blaine swung at the face with the barrel of his six-gun, but the blow was wide and the back of his fist smashed into the seamed, leathery face. Witter was knocked sprawling, and then the lineback was past and heading for the river.

A shot rang out, snapping past him, and then something hit him heavily in the side. His breath caught and he swung the lineback upstream. Then slowing down deliberately and turning up a draw, he doubled back. Every breath was a stab of pain now, but the horse was running smoothly, running as if it was his first day on the trail, and Utah turned for a glance back. Nobody was in sight. He cut up the hill and crossed the saddle into the bed of the dry wash and rode northwest toward the 46 ranch house. It was more than ten miles away, but he headed for it, weaving back and forth across the hills, using every trick he knew to cover his trail.

Twice he had to stop. Once to bandage his wound, another time for a drink. The bullet had hit him hard and he had lost blood. His saddle was wet with it and so was the side of the stallion. Turning west, he skirted the very foot of the mesa and worked toward the ranch house.

As he rode, he thought. They would know he was wounded. He mopped sweat from his face, and saw there was blood on his hand. He rubbed it against his chaps. They would know he was hurt. Now they would be like wolves after a wounded deer. He had planned to come down behind Witter, to disarm the others, then shoot it out with him. But the arrival of Lee Fox had wrecked his plans and now he was in a fix.

He walked the stallion, saving its strength. He

checked all his guns, reloading his pistol and rifle. His throat was dry and before him the horizon wavered and danced. It was hot, awfully hot. It couldn't be far to the ranch.

They were after him now, all of them. Rink Witter would now have a personal hatred. He had been struck down, and Nevers had been frightened to death. All of them . . . closing in for the kill. He tried to swallow and his throat was dry. The sun felt unbearably hot and his clothes smelled of stale sweat, and mingled with it was the sickish sweet smell of blood.

He looked down and saw the ranch close by and below him. It looked deserted. Was that a trail of dust he saw? Or were his eyes going bad on him? The heat waves danced and wavered. He turned the lineback down the trail through the woods, and he slumped in the saddle.

A last stand? No, he needed food for the run he had ahead of him. He had meant to get some from Angie, but his hunters had come too quick.

Angie . . . how dark her eyes had been! How soft and warm her lips! He had never kissed lips like them before. He remembered his arm about her waist and then he raised his head and saw that the stallion was walking into the ranch yard. He slid from the saddle. How long did he have? Ten minutes . . . a half hour . . . an hour?

They would not expect him to come here. They would never expect that. Suddenly the door on the porch pushed open and a man came down the steps. Utah Blaine stopped and squinted his eyes against the sun and the sweat. He saw Lud Fuller.

"Dumb, am I?" That was Lud's voice, all right. "I figured it right! I slipped away! Knowed you'd come here! Knowed you was bad hurt! Well, how does it feel now? Me, Lud Fuller! I'm goin' to kill Utah Blaine!"

Utah wavered and stared through the fog that hung over his eyes. This man—Lud Fuller—he had to kill him. He had to. He gathered his forces while the foreman blustered and triumphed. He stood there, swaying and watching. Fuller had a gun in his hand. Stupid the man might be, but he was not chancing a draw.

Utah Blaine got his feet planted. He smelled again the smell of his stale sweaty shirt and his unwashed body. He peered from under his flat-brimmed hat and then he said, "You're a fool, Lud! You should have gone when I sent you!"

The strength in his voice startled Fuller. The foreman stared, his eyes seemed to widen, and he pushed the gun out in front of him and his finger tightened.

He never saw Blaine draw. Blaine never knew when his hand went for the gun. There had been too many other times, too many years of practice. Wounded he might be, weary he might be, but that was there, yet, the practice and the past. And the need all deepened into a groove of habit in the convolutions of his brain. It was there, beyond the pain, the sweat and the weakness. The sure smooth flashing draw and then the buck of the gun. Fuller's one shot stabbed earth, and Utah Blaine shot twice. Both shots split the tobacco-sack tag that hung from Fuller's shirt pocket. The first shot notched it on the left, and the second shot notched it on the bottom. Swaying on his feet, Utah Blaine removed the empties and thumbed shells into his gun.

He did not look down at Fuller. In the back of his mind he remembered those brutal words when Fuller had tried to make Joe Neal die slow. Back there at the lynching—well, Fuller had certainly died fast.

Utah Blaine went into the house and he found a burlap sack in the pantry. He stuffed it with food, anything that came to hand. Then he walked out and looked in the cabinet and found some shells. He took those and put them in the sack, too. He walked out, avoiding Fuller's body and went to the corral.

A big black came toward him, whimpering gently. He put his hand out to the horse's nose, and it nudged at him. He got a bridle on the stallion and led it out. Then he switched saddles and turned the dun into the corral, but before he let the horse go he took an old piece of blanket and rubbed him off with care.

When he had finished that, and when the sack was tied behind the saddle, he bathed his wound. Still watching the trail, he took off the temporary and bloody bandage and replaced it with a new one. He was working on nerve, for he was badly hurt. Yet men had been shot up much worse and had kept moving, had survived. Nobody knew how much lead a man could carry if he had the will to live.

Somehow he kept moving, and then with the saddle on the black, he crawled aboard and started north. The river swung slightly west, he recalled. He could cross it there and get over into broken country to the northeast. As he rode he tied himself to his saddle, aware that he might not be able to stick it.

Not over three miles from the house he struck the river and crossed. There were two peaks on his left and one right of him. The rest of them were ahead. There seemed to be a saddle in front of him and

122

he started the black toward that. Then he blacked out for several miles. When he opened his eyes again, he was slumped over the saddle horn and the horse was walking steadily.

"All right, boy," he said to the horse. "You're fine, old fellow."

Reassured, the horse twitched an ear at him. The sun had set, but there was still some light. Before them the dark hollows of the hills were filled with blackness, and a somber gray lay over the land. The higher peaks were touched with reflected scarlet and gold from the sunset that still found color in the higher clouds.

All was very still. The air felt cool to his lungs and face. He held his face up to the wind and washed it as with water. His head felt heavy and his side was a gnawing agony, but before him the land was softening with velvety darkness, turning all the buffs, rusts and crimsons of the daylight desert and mountains to the quietness of night and darkness. Stars came out, stars so great in size and so near they seemed like lamps hanging only a few yards away. Off to his right lifted a massive rampart, a huge black cliff that he remembered as being in some vague account of the place told him by Neal when they traveled together. That was Deadman Mesa.

Dead man . . . he himself might soon be a dead man . . . and he had left a dead man behind him.

Dead man . . . all of them, Rink Witter, Nevers, Lee Fox and himself, all were dead men. Men who lived by violence, who lived by the gun.

Swaying in the saddle like a drunken man, he thought of that, and the names beat somberly through the dark trails of his consciousness. Rink an' Nevers an' Fox . . . Rink . . . Nevers . . . Fox

. . . all men who would die, all men who would die soon . . . Rink, Nevers, an' Fox.

The last light faded, the last scarlet swept from the sky. The dark shadows that had lurked in the lee of the great cliffs or the deepest canyons, they came out and filled the sky and gathered close around him with cooling breath and cooling arms. And the black walked on, surely, steadily, into the darkness of the night.

CHAPTER XV

BEN OTTEN hunched gray-faced in his office chair. The bank had closed hours before, but still he sat there, the muscles in his jaw twitching, his stomach hollow and empty. He had the news, what little there was. The lawyer, Padjen, was still in town. He had been retained by Neal, paid in advance, to stand by Utah Blaine.

The twenty handbills posted by Ralston Forbes had been torn from the walls by the order of Nevers, but that did not end the matter and all knew the news. Forbes was barricaded with his printer in the print shop and both men had food, ammunition and shotguns. This time they did not intend to be ejected or to have the press broken.

Mary Blake was back in town with the story of the fight at the Crossing. Rink Witter was around town with his face bandaged because of his broken nose. The smash of Blaine's fist had done that and Blaine was still alive to be hunted down. But the hunters were not having much luck. They had trailed Blaine, finally, to the 46 Connected, but once there all they found was the body of Lud Fuller, dead hours before.

Clell Miller . . . Lud Fuller . . . Tom Kelsey . . . Timm . . . how many others? And no end in sight, no end at all.

Nevers and Fox had come to the bank that morning. They had served Ben Otten with an ultimatum. They were all in it, there was no need for him to say he hadn't been. From the first he had known the score, and from the first he had lent tacit support to their plans. He had taken no active part, but the time had come. Either he came in or he was to be considered an enemy.

The prize was rich. More than three hundred thousand acres of rich range—some of it barren desert range—but the remainder well-watered and covered with grass. And the cattle. On the two ranches there must be fifty thousand head, and it was past time for a shipment. Why, there must be four or five thousand head ready for shipping right now! And a big fall shipment, too! No other range this side of the Tonto Basin would support as many cattle as this, and well Otten knew it.

If the combination won their fight, if they took over the two big outfits, they would all be wealthy men. Already two of the men who could have justly claimed shares had been eliminated. Now, if he came in, and they needed him badly, there would be but three. He could figure on a hundred thousand acres of range—more than four times what he already grazed!

All that stood between them and that wealth was one man. If Utah Blaine were killed the opposition would fall apart at the seams. For after all, Blaine had no heirs; the lawyer's part would be fulfilled, and he might take a substantial payment to leave. Mary Blake could be promised and promised and gradually squeezed out of the country with nothing or a small cash payment, which by that time she would probably need desperately.

He knew about that, for Mary Blake had no more than three hundred dollars in cash remaining in the bank.

Forbes . . . well, Ralston Forbes could be taken care of. With Blaine out of the way it would be nothing for Witter to do. And then the big melon was ready to be cut—the big, juicy melon.

Ben Otten rubbed his jaw nervously. It was a big, decision. Once actively in, he could not withdraw, and he was secretly afraid of Lee Fox. Still, the man was wild, erratic. He might get himself killed, and Nevers might, too.

Ben Otten sat up very straight. Nevers and Fox dead! That would mean . . . His lips parted and his tongue touched them, trembling. That would mean that he might have it all, the whole thing!

How to be sure they died? Of course, with Blaine in the field, anything might happen. He had his grudge against them, and he would be seeking them out soon. Blaine had killed Fuller, even though it was known that he was badly wounded. And if Utah Blaine did not? Otten remembered the cold, deadly eyes of Rink Witter . . . for cash . . . a substantial sum . . . such men were without loyalty.

He got to his feet slowly and began to pace the floor, thinking it all out. There remained Rip Coker, but the man could not live. In a pinch he would see that he did not. Yes, it was time for him to get into the game, to start moving . . . but carefully, Ben, he told himself, very, very carefully!

As he turned toward the door he had one moment of realization. It was a flashing glimpse, no more, but something about what he felt then was to remain with him, never to leave him again. He saw in one cold, bitter moment the eyes of Utah Blaine. He saw the courage of the man and the hard, driving, indomitable will of him. And he remembered Rip Coker, his back to the wall that propped him up, shooting, shooting and killing until he dropped. And Rip Coker was still clinging to a thin thread of life.

What was there in such men that made them live? What deep well of stamina and nerve supplied them? Coker had been deadly, very deadly, but at his worst he was but a pale shadow of the man known as Utah Blaine. In that brief instant with his hand on the door knob, Ben Otten saw those green, hard eyes and felt a twinge of fear. A little shiver passed through all his muscles and he felt like a man stepping over his own grave.

But the moment passed and he went on outside into the dark street. The lights from the saloon made rectangles on the street. He saw the darkness of the print shop down the street where Ralston Forbes waited with his printing press. Forbes was not through . . . what would he run off next? The stark courage of those handbills blasting Nevers and Fox was something he could admire. Forbes had nerve.

He shook his head wearily and pushed open the door to the saloon. A man turned from the bar to look at him. It was Hinkelmann, who owned the general store. As Otten moved up beside him, Hink asked, "Ben, what do you make of all this? How's it goin' to turn out? I can't figure who's right an' who's wrong."

"Well," Ben Otten agreed, "I've thought about it myself." He ordered his drink. "I've known Nevers a long time. Always treated me all right."

"Yes," Hink agreed reluctantly, "that's right."

"He pays his bills, an' I guess it rankled to see an outsider, a man with Blaine's reputation, come in here and grab off the richest ranch in the place. Although," he added, "Blaine may be in the right . . . if he and this lawyer aren't in cahoots. After all, Rink killed Neal, but who put him up to it?"

"He's workin' for Nevers," Hinkelmann suggested uneasily.

"Uh-huh, but you never know about a man like that. Offer them the cash an' . . . sometimes I've wondered just how hard they were tryin' to find Blaine. Doesn't seem reasonable one man could stay on the loose so long."

They talked some more, and after awhile, Otten left. On the steps he paused. Well, he had started it. There was still time to draw back . . . but deep within him he knew there was no time. Not any more. He was fresh out of time.

Lonely in her cabin on the river, Angie turned restlessly, wide-eyed and sleepless in her bed. Somewhere out there in the night her man was riding . . . wounded . . . bleeding . . . alone.

Her man?

Yes. Staring up into the darkness she acknowledged that to herself. He was her man, come what may, if he died out there alone; if he was killed in some hot, dusty street; if he rode off and found some other woman—he was still her man. In her heart he was her man. There was no other and there could be no other and she had felt it deep within her from that moment under the sycamores when first they talked together.

She turned again and the sheets whispered to her body and she could not sleep. Outside the leaves rustled and she got up, lighting her light and slipping her feet into slippers. In her robe she went to the stove and rekindled the fire and made coffee. Where was he? Where out there in the blackness was the man she loved?

Stories traveled swiftly in the range country and she knew all that anyone knew. She knew of the killing of Lud Fuller, of the bitter, brief struggle that preceded it and how Blaine had ridden, shooting and slashing like a madman, through the very middle of Rink Witter's killers. She had heard of Rink's smashed nose, heard of the man screaming his rage and hatred, and of how slowly Blaine would die when he got him.

She had also heard that Utah Blaine was wounded. They had followed him part of the way by the drops of blood. He had been shot, but he had escaped. Had she known where he was, she would have gone to him. Had she had any idea . . . but it was best to remain here. He knew she was here, and here she would stay, waiting for him to come to her. And so he might come.

In the morning she would ride over to the 46 and get the dun stallion. She would bring that powerful black-faced horse back here, and she would feed him well, grain him well, against the time that Blaine would come for him.

At long last she returned to bed and she slept, and in the night the rains came and thunder muttered in the long canyons, grumbling over the stones and in the deep hollows of the night.

During the day she worked hard and steadily, trying to keep occupied and not to think. She cleaned the house, cleaned every room, dusted, swept, mopped, washed dishes that had been washed and never used. She wanted to sew but when sewing she would think and thinking was something she wanted to avoid. She prepared food, put coffee out where he could find it easily if he came, and banked the fire. Then she put on her slicker and saddling her own horse, started for the 46.

She might have trouble there, but the old hands had drifted away and probably nobody would be there. She would get the dun and bring him back. She would also leave a note, somewhere where only he would be apt to find it.

The rain fell in sheets, beating the ground hard. It was not far to the 46, but the trail was slippery and she held her mare down to a walk. Rain dripped from her hat brim and her horse grew dark with it. From each rise she stopped and studied the country. The tops of the mountains were lost in gray cloud that held itself low over the hills. The gullies all ran with water and caused her to swing around to use the safest crossings.

When she saw the 46 she was startled to see a horse standing there. Even as she saw it, a man in a slicker came from the stable and led the horse inside. From the distance she could not recognize him.

Her heart began to pound. She hesitated. No one must realize that she was friendly with Blaine, and it would not do for anyone to know that she had taken the dun to her place. They would watch her at once if they did know.

Keeping to the timber, she skirted the ranch at a distance, never out of sight, watching the stable to see who would emerge. Whoever it was must soon come out and go to the house. In her mind she saw him stripping the saddle off and rubbing the water from the horse. It would be soon now, very soon.

She drew up under a huge old tree that offered

some shelter from the rain. The lightning had stopped and the thunder rumbled far away over the canyons back of Hardscrabble and Whiterock. She watched, smelling the fresh forest smells enhanced by rain and feeling the beat of occasional big drops on her hat and shoulders. Nothing happened, and then she saw the man come from the barn. Careful to leave no footprints, he kept to hard ground or rocks as he moved toward the house. There was no way to tell who it was or whether the man carried himself as if wounded.

The dun was standing with the other horses in the corral, tails to the rain, heads down. If that man had been Blaine she wanted desperately to see him. If it was not Blaine, she did not want to be seen but did want to get the dun out of the corral and away. Instinctively she knew that when Blaine could he would come to her. And when he did come she wanted his horse ready for him.

Whoever the man was, he would be watching the trail; so she started her horse and worked a precarious way down the mountain's side through the trees.

Leaving her own horse she slipped down to the side of a big empty freight wagon. Then from behind it, she moved to the stable's back. Through the window her eyes searched until they located the horse. Disappointment hit hard. Although she could not see the brand, the horse was certainly not the big stallion that Utah Blaine was reported to be riding.

The gate to the corral faced the house. There was no use trying to get the dun out that way. If she could only take down the bars to the corral . . . They were tied in place by iron-hard rawhide. She dug in her pocket for a knife and at the same time she called.

The dun's head came up, ears pricked. Then curiously he walked across to her. She spoke to him gently and he put his nose toward her inquisitively, yet when she reached a hand for him he shied, rolling his eyes. She had seen Blaine feed him a piece of bread and had come prepared, hoping it would establish them on good terms. She took out the bread and fed it to him. He took it eagerly, touching it tentatively with his lips, then jerking it from her hand.

With careful hands she stroked his wet neck, then got a hackamore on him. Knife in hand she started to saw at the rawhide thongs.

"I wouldn't," a soft voice said, "do that!"

She turned quickly, frightened and wide-eyed. Standing just behind her, gun in hand, was Lee Fox! His big eyes burned curiously as they stared at her over the bulging cheekbones of his hard, cadaverous face; the eyes of a man who was not mentally normal.

CHAPTER XVI

THE BLACK GELDING was sorely puzzled. There was a rider in the saddle but he was riding strangely and there was no guiding hand on the reins. It was the black's instinct to return home, but the rider had started in this direction and so the horse continued on. As it walked memories began to return. Three years before it had known this country. As it sensed the familiarity of the country, its step quickened.

The memory of the black was good. This way

had once been home. Maybe the rider wanted to go back. The gelding found its way through a canyon and found a vague trail leading up country between the mesa on the north and the stream that flowed from the springs.

Utah Blaine opened his eyes. His body was numb with pain and stiff from the pounding of rain. He straightened up and stared. Lightning flashed and showed him why the horse had stopped. On the right was a deep wash, roaring with flood; on the left there was the towering wall of a mesa with only a short, steep slope of talus. Directly in the trail was a huge boulder and the debris that had accompanied it in the slide.

His head throbbed and his hands were numb, and the rawhide binding his wrists to the pommel had cut into the skin. Fumbling with the knots, he got his hands loose and guided the horse forward. The narrow space between the boulder and the trail worried the gelding and it dabbed with a tentative hoof, then drew back, not liking it. "All right, old timer, we'll try the other side."

On the left was the steep slope of talus, yet at Blaine's word the horse scrambled up and around. Suddenly there was a grinding roar from above them. Frightened, the gelding lunged and Blaine, only half conscious, slid from the saddle. In some half instinctive manner he kicked loose from the stirrups and fell soddenly into the trail.

The deafening roar of the slide thundered in his ears, stones cascaded over him and then dirt and dust. He started to rise, but a stone thudded against his skull and he fell back. The dirt and dust settled, and then as if impelled by the slide, the rain roared from the sky, pelting the trail like angry hail. The black gelding, beyond the slide, waited apprehensively. The trail bothered it, and after a few minutes it started away. Behind in the trail the wounded man lay still, half-buried in mud and dirt.

When the rain pelting his face brought him out of it he turned over. Then he got to his knees, pain stabbing him. His head throbbed, and he was caked with mud and dirt. Staggering, he got over the barrier of the second slide. There was no sign of his horse and he walked on, falling and getting up, lunging into bushes, and finally crawling under a huge tree and lying there—sprawled out on the needles, more dead than alive.

There was no dawn, just a sickly yellow through the gray clouds. The black pines etched themselves against the sky, bending their graceful tops eastward. The big drops fell, and the wind prowled restlessly in the tops of the pines. Utah Blaine opened his eyes again, his face pressed to the sodden needles beneath the trees.

Rolling over, he sat up. His wound had bled again and his shirt was stuck to his side with dried blood. His head throbbed and his hair was full of blood and mud. There was a cut on his head where the stone had struck him. He felt for his guns and found them, held in place by the rawhide thongs he wore when riding.

Gingerly his fingers touched the cut and the lump surrounding it. The stone had hit him quite a belt. He struggled to get his feet under him and by clinging to the tree, hauled himself erect. His head spun like a huge top and there was a dull roaring inside his skull. Clinging to the tree, he looked around. There was no sign of the black horse.

He braced himself, then tried a step and managed to stay erect. There was a stream not far away and he made his way to the edge of it. For the time being there was no rain and he dug under a fallen log and peeled some bark from its dry side. Then he found a few leaves that were dry and a handful of grass. The lower and smaller limbs on the trees, scarcely more than large twigs, were dead and dry. These he broke off and soon he had a fire going.

When he had the flames going good he made a pot of bark and dipped up water. Then he propped the make-shift pot on a couple of stones to boil. His side was one raw, red-hot glow of agony, his head throbbed, and his body was stiff and sore. Removing his handkerchief from his neck he dried it over the fire. Then he took out his right-hand gun and cleaned it with care, wiping off all the shells. By the time that was finished, the gun returned to the holster, the water was boiling.

Soaking the bandage off the wound, he studied it as best he could. The bullet had gone through the flesh of his side just above the right hip bone, but it did not appear to have struck anything vital. His knowledge of anatomy was rusty at best. All he knew was that he had lost plenty of blood. The wound looked angry and inflamed. He began to examine the shrubs and brush close about and all he could find was the *yerba del pescado*, a plant with leaves dark on the upper side and almost white on the lower. Nearby, fortunately, he found its medicinal mate, the *yerba de San Pedro*. He ran his fingers through the leaves beneath them and found some that were partly dry. These he crushed together and placed on the wound after he had carefully bathed it. Then he rearranged the bandages as well as he could and felt better.

The sky was still somber, and he lay back, relaxing and resting. After a few minutes he put out his fire, cleaned his second gun, and got to his feet. How far he could go he did not know, but he was unsafe where he was. If the black returned home they would immediately back-track the gelding.

The mesa towering south of him would have to be Deadman, if he had kept on his course. There was no hope of escaping from the canyon now. Not with his present weakness. He would have to continue on. Walking on stones, he worked his way slowly and with many rests up along the canyon. He had to rest every fifty yards or so. But despite that, he covered some distance, his eyes always alert for a cave or other place he could use for a hideout.

Reaching a place where the talus was overgrown with brush and grass, he climbed up among the trees and continued on, keeping away from the trail. It was harder going, but he worked his way higher and higher among the rocks. After awhile he became conscious of a dull roaring sound that he was sure was not imagined. It seemed to increase and grow stronger as he pushed further along.

Coming through the trees he stopped suddenly, seeing before him a clearing with a pole corral, obviously very old, and a log cabin. Beyond it he could see a spring of white water roaring from the rocks. At the corral he could see the black gelding cropping grass. He came out of the trees and walked toward the cabin, his eyes alert. Yet he saw nothing, and when he came closer he could see no tracks nor any sign of life but the gelding.

The black horse looked up suddenly and whinnied at him. He crossed to it, stripping off the saddle and bridle and turning the gelding into the corral. Then he walked to the cabin, broke the hasp on the door and entered.

Dust lay thick over everything. There were two tiers of bunks, each three high, some benches, a chair and a table. In the fireplace there was wood as if ready for a fire and there were some pots and pans.

He walked again to the door and sat down, his rifle across his knees. Had the gelding returned to the ranch his situation would have been exceedingly precarious by now, but having come here, he knew there could be no vestige of a trail after last night's rain. Obviously nobody had been at this hideout in a long time, no doubt several years, and there was no reason to believe the place was even known of. Neal had known of it, but Neal was a close-mouthed man.

After he had rested, he got to his feet and finding an ancient broom, he swept part of the house, then lit the fire and made coffee. He had plenty of food in the pack on the gelding and he ate his first good meal in hours. Then he rested again, and when he felt better, went outside and looked carefully around. Back up in Mud Tank Draw he found another and better built shack and another corral. Further from the roaring springs, it was also more quiet, and its position was better concealed.

Catching up the gelding, which was tame as a pony, he went back to Mud Tank Draw and turned the gelding loose in that corral, then transferred his belongings to the second cabin and removed all traces of his stop at the springs. By the time he had completed this, he was physically exhausted. Rolling up in his blankets on one of the bunks, he fell asleep.

When he awakened it was night again and rain

was starting to fall. There had been an old stable outside, so donning his slicker he went out and led the gelding into a stall and pulled several armfuls of grass for him. Then he returned again to the shack, made coffee and then turned in again. Almost at once he was asleep.

He awakened with a start. It was morning and then the rain was literally pouring down on the cabin. The roof was leaking in a dozen places, but the area around the fireplace was dry. He moved to it, then broke up an old bench to get the fire hot and started coffee again.

He felt better, yet he was far from well. The wound looked bad, although it did not seem quite so flushed as before. There was no question of going out again, so he dressed the wound with some cloth from his pack and sat back in the chair.

For the first time he began seriously to consider his situation. He was wounded and weak. He had lost a lot of blood. He had ammunition and food, but shooting game to add to the larder would probably only attract attention. For the time being he believed he was safe, insofar as there could be any safety with a bloodhound like Rink Witter on his trail.

Aside from the roof, the cabin was strong and he could withstand a siege here. Yet if he were surrounded they would fire the place and he would be trapped. He would have no more chance than Nate Champion had in the Johnson County War. To be trapped in this cabin would be fatal.

For two days he rested and was secure and then on the third day he saddled the gelding and led him back up the draw at a good point for a getaway. His instinct told him that he should move, and he started back to the crevice in the rocks.

He was rolling his bed when he heard the horses.

"I tell you, you're crazy!" It was Nevers' voice. "He'd not be up here!"

"All right, then!" That was Wardlaw speaking. "You tell me where he is!"

"Boss," another voice said, "I see tracks! Somebody's been here!"

"Then it's him! Look sharp!"

Utah Blaine was through running. Dropping his rifle and bedroll he sprang into the open. "Sure, I'm here!" he shouted, and he opened fire with both hands. The rider on the paint, whoever he was, grabbed iron and caught a slug in the chest. He let go with a thin cry and started to drop. Nevers jumped his horse for the trees, firing wildly and ineffectively, and Blaine dropped another man. A slug thudded against a tree behind him and Utah yelled, "Come on Wardlaw! Here I am! Here's the thousand bucks! Come an' get it!"

The big gunman slammed the spurs to his mount and came at Utah on a dead run, but Blaine stood his ground and drove three bullets through Wardlaw's skull, knocking the man from the saddle. The horse charged down on him and Blaine, snapping a shot at the remaining man, caught up his bedroll and rifle and sprang to the saddle. He rode off up the draw, hastily swapped horses and took off swiftly.

Yet now he did not run. He circled around to the cliffs above. Three men were on the ground below and two were bent over them. As he watched, rifle in hand, Nevers came from the brush with a fourth man. That Wardlaw and at least one other man were dead, Utah Blaine knew. Now he intended to run up a score. Kneeling behind a flat rock he lifted his rifle and shot three times at Nevers. Yet he shot with no intention of killing. He wanted Nevers alive to take his defeat, at least to see the end.

A shot burned Nevers' back and he swung around staggering as the other bullets slammed about him. One of them burned him again for he sprang away, stumbling and falling headlong. One other man grabbed his stomach and fell over on the ground, and then Blaine proceeded to drive the others into the brush, burning their heels with lead and his last shot shattered a rifle stock for one of them. Reloading, he saw Nevers start to crawl and he put a shot into the ground a foot ahead of him. "Stay there, damn' you!" he yelled. "Lay there an' like it, you yellow belly!"

A rifle blasted from the brush and Blaine fired three times, as fast as he could work the lever. He fired behind the flash and to the right and left of it. He heard a heavy fall and some threshing around in the brush. He came down off the little rise and, reloading his gun as he walked, mounted the black and started back for the ranch.

He was far from good shape, he knew, but now the running was over.

Utah Blaine rode swiftly, dropping down to find a cattle trail that led to the top of Deadman Mesa. Far ahead of him he could see Twin Buttes and he rode past them. He crossed Hardscrabble and dropped down into the canyon right behind the Bench, from where Angie's ranch could be dimly seen.

Would Angie be there? Suddenly, for the first time in days, he grinned. "It would be something," he told the black gelding, "to see her again!"

He rode slowly down the trail, circled, and came up through the sycamores. There was no movement at the cabin, no smoke from the chimney. He slid from his horse and slipped the thongs back off his guns. Carefully, he walked forward, up the steps. He opened the door.

The room was empty and cold. He touched the stove. It was cold. Angie was gone. Some of the mid-day dishes were on the table, and that could only mean she had left suddenly at least one day before, possibly even prior to that.

His stomach sick with worry, he looked slowly around. Her rifle was gone. And her pistol.

He looked at the calendar. It was marked to indicate the 5th was past—this then was the sixth. She had been gone but one night. At least twenty-four hours.

Utah Blaine walked outside and looked down the trail. Beyond the hills lay Red Creek. To the northwest was the 46. Which way?

CHAPTER XVII

ANGIE KINYON looked coolly at Lee Fox. Inwardly she was far from cool, for she could see that Fox, always eccentric and queer, was now nearing the breaking point. She realized it with a kind of intuitive knowledge that also warned her the man was dangerous.

Yet Angie had heard stories about Fox. His father had been a hard-working, God-fearing pioneer, his mother a staunch woman who stood by her family. Something of that must be left in Fox.

"I want the horse," she said quietly. "It belongs to Utah Blaine."

"That's why I'm here," he replied, watching her with his strange eyes. "He'll come back for the horse."

"I doubt it. If I believed that, I wouldn't have come for him. I'm taking the horse home to be cared for. This is too fine a horse to be left like this."

Fox nodded, but she could not tell what he was thinking. Then he said suddenly, "What is he to you? What is Utah Blaine to you?"

It was in her to be frank. She looked directly at Lee Fox and spoke the truth. "I love him. I do not know whether he loves me or not. We have not had time to talk of it, but I love him the way your mother must have loved your father. I love him with all my heart."

A kind of admiration showed in the man's eyes. He laughed suddenly, and with the laughter the burning went out of his eyes. "Then he's a lucky man, Angie. A very lucky man. But let's take the stallion out the gate, no use to ruin a good corral."

It was simple as that. Something she had said, or her very honesty, had impressed Fox. He walked around the corral and roped the dun for her. She put a lead rope on him and mounted up. Fox walked to his own horse. "No need for me to stay here, then. You'll tell him." He mounted. "I'll ride with you. Nevers and his lot aren't the men to be around good women."

They rode quietly, and suddenly Fox began to talk. "You knew about my mother, then? I never knew a woman more loyal to a man. I'd admire to find her like, as Blaine has found you. Maybe after he's dead you will forget him."

"He will not die. Not now. Not of any gun this lot can bring against him."

Fox shrugged. Now he seemed normal enough.

"Maybe not, but everything's against the man. Nevers will not quit now, Otten has come off the fence, there's nowhere in this country Blaine can hope to escape. His only chance to live is to cut and run."

"And he won't do that."

"No, he won't."

He left her at the Crossing and turned away, and seemed headed for Red Creek. She sat her horse, watching him go. Would he go far or circle around and come back? That, probably. Lee Fox, sane or insane, was Western—a good woman was always to be treated with respect. He might kill her husband, brothers and son, but he would always be respectful to her.

Crossing the river, Angie rode up the far bank and turned toward the cabin in the sycamores. It was as she had left it, quiet and alone. When she had stabled the horses she went inside. Nothing was different, and it was not until she went to her dressing table and picked up her comb that she saw the note. She smiled when she saw it. Leave it to him to put the note in the place she would first come. The note read:

Stay here. Gone to 46. Back later.

"Let me see that!"

She had heard no sound. She turned, frightened, to find Rink Witter standing behind her. His hand was outstretched for the note.

Although she had known his name and his deeds for ten years, she had never seen him at close range. She looked now into the pale, almost white blue eyes, the seamed and leathery skin, the even white teeth, and the small-boned, almost delicate facial structure. She saw the hand outstretched was small, almost womanly except for the brown color. She saw the guns tied low, those guns that had barked out the last sound heard by more than one man.

Rink Witter, a scalp hunter at sixteen, a paid warrior in cattle wars at eighteen, a killer for gamblers and crooked saloonkeepers at twenty. Rustler, horse-thief, outlaw—but mostly a killer. He had ridden with Watt Moorman in the Shelbyville War. Deadly, face to face, he would kill just as quickly from hiding. He was a deadly killing machine, utterly without mercy. She had heard that the wilder the shooting, the hotter the fight, the steadier he became. He was a man who asked for no breaks and gave none.

There was no way out of it. If she did not give him the note he would take it. She would have to give it to him, play for time, watch her opportunity. Without a word, she handed the note to Rink.

He took it, studied her coolly for a minute, then read what it said.

He turned. "Hoerner," he said, "you stay here. Tell the others to head for the 46. Utah Blaine was here and he's headed there. If they don't get him there or lose his trail, they are to head for Red Creek. Tell 'em not to come back here."

Rink crumpled the note and dropped it to the floor. "Make us some coffee," he said abruptly, and then turned and picked up her rifle and pistol and walked outside.

She went to the cupboard and got out the coffee mill and ground the coffee slowly. As she worked, she tried to study this situation out. She was helpless, and getting frantic would not do a bit of good. Her only chance to help Utah was to wait, to watch, and to find some way out.

She kindled the fire and put the water on. Utah would be careful. He was too shrewd a campaigner to take chances. She must trust in that, and in his good sense. Also, he might get to the 46, find the dun gone and see her tracks.

As a matter of fact, Blaine had passed within two hundred yards of them when she was returning to the Crossing with Fox. Utah Blaine stopped under the trees near the 46 ranch house and built a cigarette. He felt better this morning. His side was sore, but he was able to move more easily. He studied the ranch house for several minutes while he smoked the cigarette. Finally decided it was deserted. He was about to leave the brush when he saw the small, sharp prints of Angie's boots. He studied the tracks, saw where she had waited under the trees as he was now doing, and then how she had circled to get behind the barn. Somebody had been at the house then.

Cautiously, he followed the trail to the corner of the corral and saw where the knife had scratched the rawhide thongs. He saw the tracks of Lee Fox, but did not recognize them at first.

There had been no struggle . . . they had walked together to the gate . . . the gate had been opened by Fox . . . the stallion led out.

He read the sign as a man would read a page of print, as a scholar or writer would read the page. He saw not only what was there, but what lay behind, interpreting movements, somehow almost discerning their thoughts, their attitudes toward each other.

The girl had mounted here . . . the man had walked to his own horse . . . a tall man or a man with very long legs. Not Witter. Not Nevers. He studied the track of the horse the tall man rode and decided: it was Lee Fox.

They had started away, riding down the trail toward the cabin. So Angie had gone home then. He must have missed them somewhere back along the trail. Or rather, he had missed them because he was not following trails.

He paused to consider this. There had to be a showdown, but he was not anxious to encounter Lee Fox, not just now. Nevers and Witter were the men he had to meet. With Fox, despite his slightly off-the-trail mind, there was a chance of reasoning. There would be none with Nevers.

Ben Otten did not enter his thinking. Otten had been out of it, and Utah Blaine had no means of knowing he had come in. Or that he could be dangerous.

He knew there was to be no more running. He was through with that now. Right was definitely on his side, and he meant to follow through on the job he had taken. He would ride right into Red Creek and show himself there. If they wanted a showdown they could have it.

He rode slowly, making it easy for the gelding. The sun was hot and dust puffed up from the horse's hoofs. He rode accompanied now by that stale smell of sweat that he would never forget after these bitter days. It seemed he had known that smell as long as he had lived, that he had always been unshaved, always gaunted from hunger, always craving cold, fresh water.

Blaine rode with ears alert for the slightest sound, his eyes roving restlessly. Yet he could not always remain alert. He could not always be careful. His lids grew heavy and his chin dropped to his chest. He lifted his head and struggled to get his eyes open. It was no use.

Turning from the mesa trail he rode down into a gulch and followed it along until he came to a patch of grass partially shaded by the sun. Lead-

146

ing his horse well back into the trees, he picketed it there. He then pulled off his boots and stretched out on the grass. No sooner was he stretched out than he was asleep.

Witter's three killers reached the 46 only a little after Blaine left. Fortunately, the three were tired, hungry, and not overly enthusiastic. They stopped to make coffee and throw together a meal from the ample stores on the 46. Only when they had eaten did they decide to pull out.

"Look," said the one named Todd, "Turley, you all stay right here. You lay for him. He might come back thisaway."

Turley had no objection. He was tired of riding. He concealed his horse and then sat down inside the house at a point from which he could see without being seen.

Now, Todd reflected, things were taking shape. With Rink Witter and Hoerner at the girl's cabin, with Turley on the 46, and with men on the Big N, they were slowly covering all the possible points of supply. Yet they lost Blaine's trail not two miles from the 46 and rode on into Red Creek to find Blaine had not been seen there. Todd then reported to Ben Otten.

Otten could see the picture clearly now, and he liked it. He had come in just at the right time. This thing was as good as ended. Fuller and Clell Miller were out of it, and he would place a small bet that either Nevers or Fox would be dead before the shooting was over. That left himself and one other to divide the pot.

"Good idea," he said, "leaving Turley at the 46. Now if Blaine goes back there he's a dead man." Otten drew a handful of coins from his pocket and

147

slapped a twenty-dollar gold piece in Todd's hand. "Buy yourself a drink," he said genially, "but not too many until this is over."

Todd pocketed the coin with satisfaction and was turning away when Ben Otten said, his voice low, "Might be a good idea, Todd, to remember where that came from. That is, if you'd like some more like it."

Todd did not turn around. "I ain't exactly a forgetful man, Mr. Otten," he said, " 'specially where money's concerned. I'll not be forgettin'. That Peebles, over yonder. He's a good man, too."

Otten drew another gold eagle from his pocket. "Give this to him, and both of you let me know how things are goin'." He hesitated, uncertain just how much to say. Then he added, "I'll want to keep in touch. When a fight like this ends nobody knows just how many will be left who can pay off."

He walked back to the bank, not knowing how much of what he had said had gotten across. Todd seemed reasonably shrewd, and he seemed ready enough to hire himself out. In any event, the forty dollars spent was little enough to insure a little good will. It might prove the decisive element. And it was better than dealing with Rink Witter. Every time he looked at the man he felt cold.

Blaine's eyes opened suddenly. The first thing he saw was a pair of huge feet and then the knees and a rifle across the knees. He looked up into the battered face of Ortmann.

Surprisingly, the big man grinned. "Man," he said, "you sleep like you fight."

"Where'd you come from?" Utah demanded, sitting up carefully. Ortmann's presence surprised him for he had not given the man a thought since their

148

fight. He knew now that he should have. Ortmann had been giving him a lot of thought.

"Been sort of lookin' around." Ortmann rubbed his cigarette into the turf. "Seen you asleep an' figured I'd better keep an eye on you. Some of Nevers' outfit went by down there, not two hours back."

"You been here for two hours?"

"Nigher to three. Figured I'd let you sleep it off."

Blaine dug for the makings and rolled a smoke. When he touched his tongue to the paper, he looked up. "What's the deal, Ort? Where do you stand?"

Ortmann chuckled and looked at Blaine with faint ironic humor. One eye was still bloodshot. "Why, no deal at all! It just sort of struck me that a man who could lick me was too good a man to die, so I figured I'd take cards."

Utah Blaine stared at him. "You mean," he said incredulously, "on my side?"

"Sure." The big man yawned and leaned back on one elbow, chewing on a chunk of grass. "Hell, I never had no fight with you. I wanted me a piece of good land, an' it figured to be easy to get some of the 46 range. The others figured the same way, although not more than five or six of them really wanted land. Some wanted trouble, some to get paid off.

"They told me you was a gunman, a killer. I decided I'd no use for you, but when you shucked your guns an' fought me my style, stand up an' knock down— Well, I decided you were my kind of folks."

Utah Blaine got to his feet and ran his fingers through his hair. Then he put on his hat and held out his hand. "Then you're the biggest big man I ever saw," he said simply, "the kind to ride the river with."

Ortmann said nothing and Blaine thought about it a minute or so. Then he said, "Now get this straight. I can use your help, but I don't want anybody else. No use getting men killed who don't need to be and sometimes too many is worse than too few. You an' me, well, we make a sizeable crowd all by ourselves." Then he added, "But how many of the others are good solid men?"

"Maybe five or six, like I said. Mostly farmers from back east, an Irish bricklayer—folks like that."

"All right," Blaine drew on his cigarette, "when this fight is over I'll see each of you settled on one hundred and sixty acres of good land. The land belongs to the ranch. You farm it on shares. The ranch will furnish the seed, you do the work. The ranch takes half of your crop. If at the end of five years you're still on the land and doin' your share, the ranch will deed the land to you."

Ortmann drew a deep breath. "Man, that's right fine! That's all right! They'll go for it, I know. And we'll have none but the best of them. I know them, every one." He picked up his rifle. "All right, Utah, where to?"

"Why to Red Creek," Blaine said quietly. "We'll go first to Red Creek."

CHAPTER XVIII

No FURTHER MOVE had been made against Ralston Forbes or his paper. Red Creek dozed in the sun with one wary eye open. All was quiet, but there were none here who did not realize that the town was simmering and ready for an explosion. Many of the citizens of Red Creek had come from Texas or New Mexico. They remembered the bitter fighting of the Moderators and the Regulators, when armies of heavily armed citizens roamed the country hunting down their enemies.

The arrival of Todd and Peebles was noticed. Both men were known. Todd had been in the Mason County War, and had escaped jail. He had broken out of jail in Sonora, too. Peebles was an Indian fighter, accustomed to killing but not accustomed to asking questions. Both were cold, hard-bitten men more interested in whiskey than in justice; their viewpoint was always the viewpoint of the man behind their hired guns.

Padjen, from his seat in front of the big window in the Red Creek Hotel, could survey the street. Skilled at acquiring information, it had taken him but a short time to get the lay of the land. He had been paid to handle any legal details about the transfer of the ranch to the hands of Utah Blaine, and he intended to see Blaine seated on the ranch securely before he left Red Creek. He witnessed the arrival of Todd and Peebles, and he was keenly interested when Todd talked with Ben Otten. He even saw the coin change hands. And he saw Todd cross to the saloon and enter, followed by Peebles.

Casually, and with all the diplomacy he could muster, the young lawyer had been moving about town and he had been talking, getting a line on sentiment and dropping his own remarks. All, he suggested, would profit if the fighting were ended. There was no telling who might be killed next. In any event, the vigilantes had been wrong to start lynching, and had been wrong in their attempts on the lives of Blake and Neal.

Actually, he suggested mildly, it looked like a factional fight in which both parties had done some shooting, but the killing of Joe Neal was out-right murder. And slowly, sentiment began to crystallize. Yet as he sat that day watching Todd and Peebles, Padjen knew that the time was far from ripe for action.

.Todd was a lean, tall man with a sour face and narrow, wicked eyes. He put his big hands on the bar and ordered a drink. Peebles, swarthy and fat faced, stood beside him. They had their drinks, then a second.

Neither man heard the two horses come into the street. But Padjen had seen them at once, and had come instantly erect. He had seen Blaine and Neal together just once, but the big man in the black hat was not hard to recognize. The huge man with him could be nobody but Ortmann.

Ducking out of the hotel he ran across the back of the building and managed to reach the livery barn as the two pulled up. Some busybody or sympathizer of the vigilante party was sure to rush at once to the two men in the saloon.

Utah Blaine saw Padjen and stopped. But as Padjen drew nearer, he recognized him instantly. "This true about Neal leavin' the ranch to me?" he asked.

"You bet it is, but watch your step or you won't inherit. Two of Witter's killers are in the saloon. Todd and Peebles."

"Bad actors," Ortmann suggested, rolling his quid in his jaws. "Which door you want me to take?"

"We'll try to take 'em prisoners," Blaine said, after a moment's thought. "There's been enough killing."

"Where'll you keep them?" Padjen asked practically. "Look, man, I'm up here to make peace if it can be done, but when you've got a rattler by the tail you'd best stomp on his head before he bites you."

"Makes sense," Ortmann agreed.

Utah Blaine turned the problem over in his mind, then looked at Padjen. "Is Angie Kinyon in town?"

"No," the lawyer said, "she's not. I've never met her but if she was here, I'd know it. Mary Blake knows her."

Had Angie returned to the ranch? If so, where was Rink Witter? Utah considered the possibilities and liked none of them. Not even a little bit. And there was this affair, here in town. "Better get back to the hotel," he advised Padjen. "No use you getting into this."

"But I—" Padjen started to protest.

"No," Blaine was positive, "you'll do more good on the sidelines."

Padjen started back up the street but when he had gone only a few steps and was crossing the street, Todd came from the door of the saloon. He stood there, one hand on the doorway, staring at Padjen. The innate cruelty of the man wanted a victim, and here, in the person of this city lawyer who had brought the news to Utah Blaine, he decided he had found his man.

"You!" Todd walked out from the awning. "Come over here!"

Padjen felt his stomach grow cold. He was wearing no gun, and had little skill with one. Yet he walked on several steps before he stopped. "What is it?" he asked quietly. "Are you in need of an attorney?"

Todd laughed. "What the hell would I want with a lawyer? I never do no lawin'. I settle my arguments with a gun."

153

"You do? Then you'll need to be defended sometime, my friend," Padjen smiled. "Unless a lynch mob gets to you sooner."

Todd stepped down off the walk and walked toward Padjen. Behind him a door closed and he knew Peebles had come out. "Run him my way, Todd," Peebles said. "I'll put a brand on him."

Padjen's face was pale, but he kept his nerve. "Better not start anything," he said quietly. "Ben Otten wouldn't like it."

That stopped Todd and puzzled him. This man had brought news of Blaine's inheritance to town. On the other hand, he was a lawyer and it was Todd's experience that lawyers and bankers were thicker than thieves. The change of the gold piece rattled in his pocket and he wanted to do nothing to stop that flow of gold, now that it was started.

"What you got to do with Ben Otten?"

Padjen perceived his advantage. The outlaw was puzzled and a little worried. "That," Padjen said sharply, "is none of your business. If Ben wants to tell you anything, that's his problem. Not mine. Now stand aside."

Drawing a deep breath he walked on, and in a dozen steps, forcing himself to an even pace, he got to the hotel. He turned in and stopped, leaning weakly against the wall. He looked at the gray-haired clerk. "That," he said, "was close!"

But the situation in the street had not ended. Irritated by his loss of a victim and the inner feeling that he had been tricked as well as frustrated, Todd looked for a new target. He saw a man standing in the center of the street not fifty yards away.

This man was tall, the flat brim of his black hat shaded the upper part of his face. The man wore a sun-faded dark blue shirt, ragged and stained.

Twin gunbelts crossed his midsection and he wore two guns, low and tied down. His boots were shabby and had seen a lot of weathering since their last coat of polish. He did not recall ever having seen this man before.

As he looked, the silent figure began to move. The tall man walked slowly up the street and Todd, with just enough whiskey in him to be mean, hesitated. There was something about that man that he did not like the looks of. He squinted his eyes, trying to make out the face, and then he heard Peebles.

"Watch it!" Peebles' whisper was hoarse. "That's Utah Blaine!"

Shock stiffened Todd and momentarily he floundered mentally. Todd had never claimed to be a gunfighter of Blaine's class. He was a hired killer, good enough and always ready enough to kill. He was not lacking in courage for all his innate viciousness. On the other hand, he was no damned fool.

Blaine came on, straight toward him, saying nothing. It was Todd who broke first. "What you want? Who are you?"

"You ride with Witter. You've been huntin' me. I'm Blaine."

Todd swallowed. That was the signal, and he should have gone for his gun. Suddenly the sun felt very hot and he began to sweat. Suddenly he wondered what he was doing here in this street. What did he want to start trouble for when he could be in the saloon. Why had he not stayed there?

"I ain't huntin' you."

"Seemed mighty anxious back at the Mud Tank," Blaine said. "Well, you've got a choice. Drop your guns and take the next train out of town—or you can die right here."

There it was, right in his teeth. Somehow he had

always known this moment would come: the show-down he could not avoid. Yet it had been a noose he feared more than a bullet. Maybe he was lucky.

Blaine raised his voice. "That goes for you, too, Peebles. Drop your gunbelt right where you are and get out of town on the next train."

That did it. Peebles was standing at the door of the saloon. He thought he had a chance. There was no loyalty in the man and if Blaine fired it would be at Todd. In that split second he might kill Utah Blaine and collect that thousand dollars Nevers offered.

In that stark instant of hesitation before Peebles replied, Todd saw with a queer shock, an intuitive sense that told him what the move would be.

"You don't scare me, Blaine!" Peebles' words rang loud. "I'm not leavin' town an' I'm not droppin' my guns!" As he spoke, his hand dropped to his gun.

Todd had seen it coming. He reached. Both hands dropped . . . he felt the solid, comfortable grasp of the gun butts . . . his fingers tightened . . . something smashed him in the stomach, and for an instant he believed Blaine had swung a fist at him. But there was Blaine, still at least twenty yards away. Another something ran a white hot iron through his body. Todd stared down the street and the figure of the man in the black hat wavered . . . somewhere another gun blasted . . . the figure wavered still more and he withdrew his gaze, looking down at the gray dust at his feet. That was odd! There were big, red drops, bright, gleaming drops on the dust . . . red . . . blood . . . but whose . . . he looked down at himself and a queer, shaking cry went through him. He looked up, staring at Blaine. "No!" he exploded in a deep, gasping cry.

'Please! Don't shoot!" And then he fell forward on his face and was dead.

Peebles had snapped a quick shot, missed and lost his nerve. He saw Todd take it in the belly and he wheeled, springing for the door. He would take his second shot from safety, he would . . . he burst through the doors and stopped.

Ortmann had come in the back door of the saloon. He was standing in the middle of the room with a shotgun in his hands. "Howdy, Peebl!" he said. "You shot at a friend of mine!"

"I got nothin' to do with you!" Peebles said hoarsely. Behind him was Blaine, and Blaine would be coming. Desperation lent him courage and he swung his pistol at Ortmann. His shot missed by a foot, smashing a bottle on the back bar. Ortmann's solid charge of buckshot smashed him in the stomach. Peebles hit the doors hard, spun around them as if jerked by a powerful hand. He hit the boardwalk hard, throwing his gun wide. His eyes opened, closed, then opened again. It was cool in the shadow under the porch. So . . . cool . . .

Padjen mopped his face. Not three minutes had passed since Todd had stopped him, and now two men were dead. He saw Blaine feed shells into his gun and then turn and walk up the street.

Ben Otten was sitting behind his desk. He had heard the shooting but did not get up. He was not anxious to know what was happening right now, the less one was around at such times the better. And someone would come and tell him.

Blaine told him.

When the door closed, Ben Otten looked up. He saw Utah Blaine standing there and he swallowed hard. "What—why— Howdy, Utah! Somethin' I can do for you?"

"Yes. You can pack up an' leave town."

"Leave town?" Otten got up. "You can't be talkin' to me, Blaine! Why, I—you can't get away with that—I own this bank—I've a ranch—I've—" His voice stuttered away and stopped.

"You're in this up to your ears, Ben." Blaine was patient. "You're a plain damn fool, buckin' a deal like this at your age. You pack up an' get out."

Otten fought for time . . . time to think, to plan . . . any kind of time . . . any amount. "What happened down the street?" he asked.

"Todd and Peebles bucked out in gunsmoke."

"You . . . you killed 'em?"

"Todd. Ortmann killed Peebles."

"Ortmann?" The banker wiped a hand across his mouth. "What's he got to do with Peebles?"

"Ortmann's with me." Blaine watched Otten take that and was coldly satisfied at the older man's reaction. "And get this straight," Blaine's voice was iron-hard. "When I tell you to leave town, I mean it. When I've straightened things out with Rink Witter, Nevers and Fox, then I'll come for you. I hope you're not here, Otten."

Ben Otten's diplomacy had worn thin. His fear was there, right below the surface. He felt it, knew it for what it was, and was angered by it. He felt his nostrils tighten and knew he would be sorry for this, but he said it. "You've taken on a big order, Utah. Witter, Nevers an' Fox—then me. You may never get to me."

"Don't bank on it." Utah leaned his big hands on the rail. "If there's one thing I've no use for, Ben, it's a man who straddles the fence waitin' for the game to be killed before he rushes in to pick over the carcass—an' all the time hopin' he'll be the only one to get the fat meat.

158

"You're not a smart man, Ben. I've learned that in just a few days by what I've seen and what I've heard. You've got a few dollars, some mortgages on property and a big opinion of yourself. Don't let that big opinion get you killed. Believe me, a small man enjoys his food just as much—and lives a lot longer."

He turned abruptly and walked from the bank. He was suddenly tired. Pausing on the street he built a smoke, taking his time. He had been left a heritage that made him a wealthy man. But the heritage carried with it the responsibility of holding it together, building something from it. With a kind of sadness he knew his old foot-loose days were over, yet he accepted the responsibility and understood what it meant.

There could be war here, but there could be peace. But somebody had to accept the responsibility of keeping that peace, and he knew that task was his.

Ortmann was standing down the street, waiting for him. He grinned as Blaine came up. "We do better fightin' together than each other," he said grinning.

Blaine chuckled. "You punch too hard, you big lug. And you sure used that shotgun right."

"I knowed Peebles. He's a sure-thing killer, a pot-hunter. Killed maybe a dozen men, but maybe one or two had a chance at him." He fell into step with Blaine. "What now?"

Blaine stopped at the newspaper office and Ralston Forbes stepped out to meet him. Padjen was coming down the street. "I want you to get out a paper, Rals," Utah said, "and give me some space on the front page. I'll buy it if need be."

"You won't have to. Anything you say around here is front page news."

"All right." Utah threw his cigarette into the dust and rubbed it out with his toe. "Then say this: As of noon tomorrow I am takin' over the 46 Connected. I'll be hirin' hands startin' Monday an' want twenty men for a roundup. Say that Nevers has ten days to sell out and get out. In that time if I see him, I'll shoot him."

"You want to publish *that?*" Padjen exclaimed.

"Exactly. Also," Blaine continued, "inform Fox that I want any stock of his off 46 range within that same ten days. That so far as I am concerned, he's out of it if he keeps himself out."

"He won't," Ortmann said.

"Maybe, but there's his out." Blaine drew a breath. "Now we've got a job. We're goin' to the 46 tonight."

CHAPTER XIX

IT WAS Ben Otten who carried the news to Nevers on the Big N. "So he's goin' back to the 46, is he?" Nevers mused. "Well, he won't last long there."

Ben Otten was heavy with foreboding. He had been given his walking papers by Blaine, but of that he said nothing to Nevers. The only thing that could save him now would be the death of Utah Blaine, and a sense of fatality hung heavily around him. Nevers' confident tone failed to arouse him to optimism.

"Who's on the 46?"

"Turley. Rink and Hoerner are on the girl's place."

Otten got up restlessly. "That's bad! Folks won't stand for any botherin' of women. You know that

Nevers. I think some of my own hands would kill a man who bothered her."

"She's safe with Rink. He's mighty finicky around women. But," Nevers looked at Otten, his eyes glistening, "I'm goin' over there myself. That filly needs a little manhandlin'. She butted into this. Now she'll get what she's askin' for."

"Leave that girl alone!" Otten's voice was edged. "I tell you folks won't take it!"

"Once we're in the saddle who can do anythin' about it? Anyway, it'll be blamed on Blaine. Everythin' will."

There was no talk of Angie Kinyon doing any talking herself. Evidently Nevers didn't intend to leave her alive to do any talking. Ben Otten was shocked and he stared at Nevers. How far the man had come! A few weeks ago he had been ranching quietly and looking longingly at the rich miles of 46 grass. First the lynching, then the killing of Gid Blake, and the attempt on Neal. Whose idea had it been? Partly Nevers' and partly Miller's, he seemed to remember. But the step from killing a man and stealing his ranch to murdering a woman was a small one apparently.

He rubbed his jaw, thinking of Angie alone . . . and Nevers. Otten began to sweat.

Nevers went out and slammed the door behind him. Otten looked at the shotgun on the rack . . . Ortmann used a shotgun. He would be blamed . . . He hesitated, remembering the light in the bunkhouse. Anyway, why should he kill Nevers? To protect Angie . . . or to save her for himself?

His mouth grew dry and he gulped a cup of water, then walked to the bunkhouse. A sour-faced oldster whom he knew only by sight sat on the bunk reading. Another man was asleep on a cot.

161

Three bunks within the range of light held no bedding at all. Otten looked at these bunks, then indicated them with a nod of his head. "Some of the hands take out?"

"Yep. Three of 'em pulled their freight this mornin'. Don't know's I blame 'em."

"Why?"

"Big N's finished." There was something fatalistic in the old cowhand's voice. "When Nevers took to buckin' Blaine, he was finished. It's in the wind."

"He's only one man."

"An' what a man. Look what's happened. All of 'em after him. He rides over to Yellowjacket an' whips that big bruiser of an Ortmann. Whips him to a frazzle.

"All of you again' him. Nevers, you, Fox, Miller, Fuller an' Rink Witter. Well, he's out-guessed all of you. Miller's dead. Lud Fuller is dead. Wardlaw is dead. Two, three others are dead. Now Todd an' Peebles are dead—an' they were hard men, believe you me. But is Blaine dead? Not so's you'd notice it."

"He's been lucky."

The oldster spat. "That ain't luck, that's savvy. Once it might o' been luck, twict it might have been, but Blaine has just out-guessed an' out-figured you ever' jump. He just thinks an' moves too fast for you. Besides, this here row's goin' to blow the lid off. Too bloody. The law will come in here an' you fellers ain't got a leg to stand on. Not a bit of it, you ain't."

The truth of this did not make it more acceptable. Otten turned away irritably. Nevers' own hands were deserting him. He walked back to his horse and stood there, weighted down by a deep sense of desolation.

The thought of Nevers alone with Angie came to his mind again. God! What a woman she was! He remembered the easy way she moved, the line of her thigh against her dress when she rode, the whiteness of her throat at her open neck, the swell of her breasts beneath ... He swung into the saddle and jerked the horse around savagely. Suddenly, he slammed his spurs into the gelding.

He'd get there only a few minutes behind him. He'd stop Rink. He would get Rink or Nevers. He would ... he would kill Nevers himself. Himself ... and then ... and then ... Viciously he jammed the spurs into the mare and went down the trail with the wind cutting his face.

He took the trail across Bloody Basin at a dead run. He would get there before Nevers could ... He settled down to hard, wicked riding. Something warned him he was going to kill the horse, but he was beyond caring.

In Red Creek Ralston Forbes looked across the restaurant table at Mary Blake. They had been much together these past days. Yet now Forbes was restless. The whole country was alive with suspense and if he ever saw a powder keg ready to blow up, this country was it. Twice within the past hour he had seen men he knew as sober citizens walking down the street, wearing guns and carrying rifles or shotguns. Things were getting stirred up.

"Otten rode out of town," Mary told him.

"He's in it. Right up to his ears. Somebody talked an' I've got a list of that lynch crowd. Lud Fuller was the leader, but Otten was with them just before they killed your father. He met them right afterward, too. So soon after that I know he was close by. He was just trying to be smart and keep his skirts clean."

"Dad always thought Otten was his friend."

"The man's money-hungry. It's an obsession now. And there is none worse. It makes a man lose perspective. It's the getting that's important, the getting and having—not how it's gotten."

"What's it come to, anyway, Rals?"

"Honor should mean more." Forbes shrugged. "Sometimes I think people have gone crazy. The size of this country, the richness of it—it seems to drive them into a sweat to get all they can, to fight, kill, connive—so many have forgotten any other standard. Not all, fortunately, the country breeds good men and it will breed better. All these others, they'll burn themselves out someday, expand so fast they run up against the edges and die there. Then the good men will reconstruct. It's the advantage of having youth in a country, and a government that is pliable and adjustable to change."

Padjen came in as they sat there. He bowed to Mary, then drew up a chair and seated himself. "I've been approached," he said, "by a half-dozen of the townsmen. They want me to help them hold an election and choose a mayor, a city council, and a marshal."

"I'm for it," Forbes slapped his hand on the table. "It's long overdue."

"Who for marshal?" Padjen inquired. "You know these men. I wanted Blaine, but they wouldn't go for that."

"You wouldn't expect them to. He's one side of the argument." Forbes considered it. "I'd roust out Rocky White."

"Wasn't he a Big N cowhand?"

"He's worked for all of them, Neal, Nevers and

164

Otten. But he's a good man, and he's a man who will take the job seriously. And he's not a killer."

"All right."

"What will happen now, Rals? Won't this make trouble for Utah, too?"

"It may, but even he would be for it. There's got to be an end to this shooting and killing."

They were silent, Ralston Forbes staring at the plate before him, his face somber. Mary looked across the table at him, moving uneasily in her chair. "What will they do, Rals?" she asked. "Will they arrest Blaine, too?"

"I don't know. All of them—they are aroused. I could see it coming. They've nothing against Blaine. They know he didn't start it, and they realize his claim to the 46 is just and legal. But his reputation is against him. After all, he's a gunfighter and known as one."

"Have you seen Rip?" she asked then.

"He's a little better. He had his eyes open today and was conscious when they fed him. He went right off to sleep again."

Mary Blake got to her feet. "Rals, I'm worried about Angie. She's out there on that ranch. A few weeks ago I'd not have worried. But the way things are, anything might happen."

He rubbed the back of his neck and nodded. "Yes, we were talking about her. Padjen and I." He walked restlessly down the room while Mary waited. All her animosity for Angie was gone. It had been a transient thing, born of her sudden need for the strong hands and will of Utah Blaine and her need for the ranch—the need for revenge for her father's murder.

Now, since she had been so much with Rals Forbes, her feelings had changed. He was like

Blaine, but different. Without Blaine's drive and fury, without some of his strength, but with a purpose behind his will that was equally definite.

"We'll get a posse, Padjen," Forbes said suddenly, "we'll ride out there."

"Wait a minute. No use to go off half-cocked. I've sent for Rocky White."

There was silence in the room. The waiter came in and refilled their coffee cups. Forbes was somber and lonely in his thinking, Padjen absorbed. After a few minutes Kent, who owned a general store, came in. With him was Dan Corbitt, the blacksmith, and Doc Ryan.

Rocky White came at last. He was a tall, rawboned young man with a serious face and strong hands. "This right?" He looked around. "You want me for town marshal?"

"That's right." Forbes did the talking. "We've met and agreed that you're the man for the job. You run things here in town. See the violence stops, guns are checked upon entry of the town limits. No fighting, no damaging of property, protection for citizens."

"How about outside of town?"

"I was coming to that. Angie Kinyon is out there on her place. It isn't safe. We're going out there to get her. If we run into any fighting we'll stop it and make arrests. We'll bring Angie back here."

White nodded slowly. Then he looked around. "My pa was a J.P., and he was sheriff one time. I reckon I know my duties, but you better understand me. I'll kill nobody where it can be avoided. I'll make peaceful arrests when I can—but when I can't, will you back me?"

"To the hilt!" Kent said emphatically. "It's time we had law and order here!"

Forbes nodded agreement as did the others. Then Rocky White looked around. "One more thing. What about Utah Blaine?"

"What about him?"

"He's right friendly with you, Forbes. An' I understand Padjen here represents him legally. I'll play no favorites. If he has to be arrested, I arrest him, too."

Forbes nodded. "That's right."

White shifted his feet. "Understand me. I've no quarrel with Blaine. I quit my ridin' job because I believed he was right. I still believe it. There was no call to grab all that range, an' Blaine had a right to fight for it. However, if we can make peace at all, it will have to include him."

"Right."

Rocky White shoved back from the table. "Then we'll ride."

Turley fixed a meal and ate it, then rousted around until he found a bottle of whiskey. Pouring himself a drink, he walked out to the veranda where he could watch the trail in both directions. He had been on the ranch for several hours and he was restless. He wanted to know what was going on.

He sat on the porch drinking whiskey and smoking, his eyes alert. A thousand dollars for killing Blaine —it was more money than he had ever had in his life. And Blaine would probably come here, to the 46.

Returning to the kitchen, he picked up the bottle and walked back through the house to the porch again. His eyes drifted toward the trail and stopped, his brow puckered. Was that dust?

Rifle in hand he walked to the edge of the porch,

then came down the steps. He had heard no sound. If it was dust there was little of it. Maybe a dust devil.

The incident made him nervous. It was too quiet here. He held his rifle in his hands and looked slowly around the ranch yard. All was very still.

"Hell," he said aloud, "I'm gettin' jumpy as a woman."

Rifle in the crook of his arm he strolled down to the corral and forked hay to the horses. He watched them eating for several minutes, then turned and walked lazily back to the shelter of a huge tree. He sat down on the seat that skirted the tree, his eyes searching the edge of the woods, the corners of the buildings—everywhere. Nothing.

It was unlike him to be nervous. He got up again and started for the house. A noise made him turn. Nothing. A leaf brushed along the ground ahead of some casual movement of air. Irritably, he started again for the house and mounted the steps. He opened the door of hide strips and seated himself in the cool depths of the porch.

He poured another drink. Warmth crept through his veins and he felt better. Much better. Suddenly, he got up. Why the hell hadn't they left somebody here with him? It was still as death. Not even a bird chirping . . . not a quail.

The cicadas were not even singing their hymn to the sun. A horse stamped and blew in the corral. Turley passed his hand over his face. He was sweating. Well, it was hot. He poured another drink . . . good whiskey . . . he placed the glass down and looked carefully around, eyes searching the edge of the trees. All was quiet, not a leaf moved.

Suddenly he heard a sound of a horse on the trail. It was coming at a canter. He got up hastily and walked to the edge of the porch, then down the steps. The horse was still out of sight among the trees. Then the horse came nearer, passed the trees and was behind the stable. Then it rounded the stable and rode up in the yard. Turley could not get a glimpse of the man's face under his hat brim. The man swung down and trailed the reins. He stepped around the horse and Turley stared. It was Utah Blaine.

Turley was astonished. He had never for an instant doubted the rider was a friend. No other, he reasoned, would ride into the yard so calmly. But here it was. He had wanted Blaine's scalp, wanted that thousand dollars— Here it stood! A tall man with two good hands and two guns that had killed twenty men or more.

"You're Turley?"

It was an effort to speak. Turley's throat was dry. "Yeah, I'm Turley."

"A couple of friends of yours came out on the short end of a gun scrap in Red Creek, Turley. Todd an' Peebles."

"Dead?" Turley stared uneasily, wishing he was still back on the porch. The sun was very hot. Why had he drunk that whiskey? A man couldn't be sure of his movements when he was drinking. "You kill 'em?"

"Only Todd. Peebles tried to make a sure thing of it from a doorway but there was a man behind him with a shotgun. Ortmann was back there. Nearly tore Peebles in two."

"Why tell me?" Turley was trying to muster the nerve to lift his rifle. Could he move fast enough?

"Figured you'd like to know, Turley," Blaine said softly. "It might keep you alive. You see, Ortmann is behind you right now, an' holding that same shot-gun."

Cold little quivers jumped the muscles in the back of Turley's neck as Ortmann spoke. "That's right, man. An' I'm not in line with Blaine. Want to drop your guns or gamble? Your choice."

Turley was afraid to move. Suppose they thought he was going to gamble? Suddenly, life looked very bright. He swallowed with care. "I never bucked no stacked deck," he said. "I'm out of it."

Carefully, he dropped his rifle, then his belt gun. He looked to Blaine for orders.

"Get on your horse, Turley," Blaine said, "an' ride. If you ever show around here again we'll hang you."

Turley was shaken. "You—you're lettin' me go?"

"That's right—but go fast—before we change our minds."

Turley broke into a stumbling run for his horse. Pine . . . that was where . . . he would head for Pine . . . then south and east for Silver City. Anywhere away from here . . .

CHAPTER XX

ANGIE was frightened and she was careful. There was an old pistol, a Navy revolver her father had left behind him. It was on a shelf in a closet, in a wooden box, and fully loaded. Her awareness of the gun did a little to ease her fear, yet she made no move to get it. She had no good place to conceal the weapon and did not want to go for it until the move was absolutely essential.

She had taken the measure of Rink Witter within a few hours after his arrival. He treated her with a deference that would have been surprising had she not known Western men. Rink was a Westerner —utterly vicious in combat, ruthless as a killer, yet with an innate respect for a good woman.

Hoerner was not of this type. Angie also knew that. When she fixed her hair she deliberately dressed it as plainly as possible and did what she could to render herself less attractive. The task was futile. She was a beautiful girl, dark-eyed and full of breast with a way of walking that was as much a part of her as her soft, rather full lips.

Hoerner was a big man, hair-chested and deep of voice. His eyes followed her constantly, but she knew that as long as Rink was present, 'she was safe. Nor would Hoerner make the slightest move toward her when Rink was around. The gunman was notoriously touchy, and Hoerner was far too wise to risk angering him.

Rink Witter was possessed of an Indian-like patience. Blaine's note had said he would be back and without doubt he would be. Rink sensed that Angie Kinyon was in love with Utah, and he respected her for it. Despite the fact that he intended to kill Blaine, and would take satisfaction in so doing, he was an admirer of the man. Utah Blaine was a fighter, and that was something Rink could appreciate.

When he saw the dust on the trail he did not rise. He sat very still and watched. Yet he knew, long before the man's features or the details of his clothing were visible, that it was not Blaine. This angered him.

Whoever it was, the rider should not be coming here. There was no reason for anyone coming here. The dust or tracks might worry Blaine into being overly cautious. And Rink expected Utah to take no chances, but now he became bothered.

The rider was Nevers. He rode into the yard and swung down from his horse. Rink came to his feet and swore softly, bitterly. Nevers was headed for the door, having left the horse standing there in the open! The fool! Who did he think Utah was, a damn' tenderfoot?

Nevers pushed open the door, looking quickly around for Angie. "Where's that girl?" he demanded.

"Other room." Rink jerked his head. "What's the matter? You gone crazy? If Blaine saw that horse he'd never ride in here."

"Blaine's headed for the 46. That's the place to get him. You and Hoerner get on over there."

Rink did not like it. He did not like any part of it. "He's comin' here. He left a note."

"That doesn't make any difference. Otten saw him in town. He told Ben he was takin' the 46 into camp. That he was movin' on and wasn't goin' to move off."

That made sense, but still Rink did not like the setup. Nor did he like Nevers' manner. What was wrong he could not guess, but something was. Then he thought of another thing. "Otten saw Blaine in town? Where were my men?"

Nevers restrained himself with impatience. To tip his hand now would be foolhardy. Rink would never stand for anything like he had in mind. "Your men?" Despite himself his voice was edged with anger. "A lot of good they did! Blaine an' Ortmann wiped 'em out. Blaine killed Todd an' when Peebles tried to cut in, Ortmann took him."

That demanded an explanation of Ortmann's presence with Blaine. Nevers replied shortly, irritably. Hoerner watched him, smoking quietly. Hoerner was not fooled. He could guess why Nevers was here and what he had in mind.

172

Rink hesitated, searching for the motivation behind Nevers' apparent anxiety or irritation. He failed. He shrugged. "All right, we'll go to the 46. Turley's there. If Blaine rides in, Turley should get one shot at him, at least."

Rink turned and jerked his head at Hoerner. The big man hesitated, looking at Nevers. "You sure you want me?" he asked softly. "Maybe I'd better stay here."

Nevers' head swung and he glared at Hoerner. "You ride to the 46!" he said furiously. "Who's payin' you?"

"You are," Hoerner said, "long as I take the wages. Maybe I aim to stop."

Rink Witter stared from one to the other. "You comin' with me?" he asked Hoerner. "Or are you scared of Blaine?"

Hoerner turned sharply, his face flushing. "You know damn' well I'm scared of nobody!" He caught up his hat and rifle. "Let's go!" At the door he paused. "Maybe we'll be back mighty soon," he said to Nevers.

Nevers stood in the doorway and watched them go. Then he turned swiftly. Angie Kinyon stood in the door from the kitchen. "Oh? Have they gone?"

"Yeah." Nevers' voice was thick and something in its tone tingled a bell of warning in Angie's brain.

She looked at him carefully. She had never liked Nevers. He was a cold, unpleasant man. She could sense the animal in it, but it had nothing of the clean, hard fire there was in Utah Blaine. Nevers' neck was thick, his shoulders wide and sloping. He stared across the table at her. "You get into a man, Angie," he said thickly. "You upset a man."

"Do I?" Angie Kinyon knew what she was facing now, and her mind was cool. This had been something she had been facing since she was fourteen, and there had always been a way out. But Russ Nevers was different tonight—something was riding him hard.

"You know you do," Nevers said. "What did you want to tie in with Blaine for?"

"Utah Blaine's the best man of you all," she said quietly. "He stands on his own feet, not behind a lot of hired gunmen."

Red crept up Nevers' neck and cruelty came into his eyes. He wanted to get his hands on this girl, to teach her a lesson. "You think I'm afraid of him?" he demanded contemptuously. Yet the ring of his voice sounded a little empty.

"I know you are," Angie said quietly. "You're no fool, Russ Nevers. Only a fool would not be afraid of Blaine."

He dropped into a chair and looked across the table at her. "Give me some of that coffee," he commanded.

She looked at him, then walked to the stove and picked up the pot. Choosing a cup, she filled it. But instead of coming around the table as he had expected, she handed it across to him. He tried to grasp her wrist and she spilled a little of the almost boiling coffee on his hand.

With a cry of pain he jerked back the hand, pressing it to his lips. "Damn' you! I think you done that a-purpose!"

"Why, Mr. Nevers! How you talk!" she mocked.

He glared at her. Then suddenly he started around the table. "Time somebody took that out of you!" he said. "An' I aim to do it!" Swiftly she evaded his grasp and swung around the table.

"You'd look very foolish if somebody came in,"

she said. "And what would you do if Blaine rode up?"

He stopped, his face red with fury. Yet her words somehow penetrated his rage. At the same time he realized that he had deliberately separated himself from all help! Suppose Blaine did come?

Coolly, Angie took the note she had picked up from where Rink had thrown it. She tossed it across the table. "How does that make you feel?" she asked. "You know what would happen if Blaine found you trying to bother me."

"He won't find us," he said thickly. "They'll get him at the 46!"

Yet even as they talked several things were happening at once. Ben Otten was racing over the last mile to the cabin on the river, while Lee Fox, with two riders, was closing in from the north. He had left his post, watching for Blaine, and had taken a brief swing around through the hills. Reining in, at the edge of the trees, he looked down and saw the horse standing in the yard. And then he saw a second rider come racing down to the ford and start into the river. Lee Fox spoke quickly and rode down the trail.

In Red Creek six deputies with shotguns were stationed at six points in the town. Their job was to keep the peace. Before the hotel fifteen men were mounted and waiting. And then Rocky White came out, followed by Padjen and Forbes. All mounted.

A tough gunhand who had come drifting into the valley hunting a job, filled his glass. He looked over at the bartender. "One for the road!" he said.

"You leavin'?"

The gunhand jerked his head toward the street. "See them gents ridin' out of town? Those are good people, an' they are mad, good an' mad! Mister, I been in lots of scraps, but when the average folks get sore, that's time to hit the trail! Ten minutes an' you won't see me for dust!"

Ben Otten raced up the trail just as Nevers started after Angie the second time. Nevers stopped just as she reached the door into the next room. He stopped and heard the pound of hoofs. His face went blank, then white. He grabbed for a gun and ran to the door. He was just in time to see a man swing down from a horse and lunge at the steps. Nevers was frightened. He threw up his gun and pulled it down, firing as he did so.

Ben Otten saw the dark figure in the door, saw the gun blossom with a rose of fire, and felt something slug him in the stomach. His toe slipped off the first step and he fell face down, and then rolled over and over in the dust.

Russ Nevers rushed out, his gun lifted for another shot. He froze in place, staring down at the fallen man.

Ben Otten!

Angie heard his grunt of surprise, but she was pulling the box down from the shelf of the closet. Lifting out the gun she concealed it under her apron and walked back to the kitchen.

Russ Nevers was on the steps and he heard her feet. He turned, staring blankly at her. "It's Otten," he said dully. "I've killed Ben Otten."

He was still staring when Fox rode into the yard with his men. He looked down at Otten, then at Nevers. "What did you shoot *him* for?" he asked wonderingly.

"He rushed me. I thought he was Blaine."

Fox peered peered at Nevers curiously, then

176

looked up at Angie. Slowly realization broke over him, and he looked from one to the other, then nodded, as if he had reached a decision.

"Get him out of the way," he said shortly. "Blaine's comin'." He turned to his men. "Gag that girl, but be easy on her."

Angie heard him speak, but not the words. The two men swung down as Nevers caught Otten's body by the arm to drag it aside. The two hands walked toward her, apparently about to help Nevers. She did not suspect their purpose until suddenly they grabbed her. She tried to swing up the gun but it was wrested from her.

"You won't be hurt," Fox said. "We just don't want you to warn Utah."

Helplessly, she watched them scatter dust over the blood where Ben had fallen. She watched them lead the horses away and scatter dust over their tracks. She watched them carefully take their positions.

Russ Nevers inside the house . . . Lee Fox in the stable . . . his two riders, one in the corral and one behind a woodpile near the edge of the timber. There they were: five men and all ready to kill. And somewhere along the trails were Rink Witter and Hoerner.

Utah Blaine had been gone for more than twenty minutes when Ortmann heard the riders coming. He got a glimpse of them right away: Rink Witter and Hoerner.

Taking his time he drew a careful sight on Hoerner and fired. The shot was a miss, but it frightened the two and both of them jumped their horses into the brush. Coolly, using a rifle, Ortmann began to spray the brush, working his way across and then back, and jumping a shot from time to time.

Hoerner was flat on his face in the brush, hugging the ground. The bullets overhead had a nasty sound. "That ain't Utah!" he said. "He'd have let us come closer!"

"I know it ain't. Must be Ortmann."

"What are we waitin' for? Let's get back. Blaine's sure to go gal-huntin' now."

Rink Witter thought it over and decided Hoerner was right. Moreover, he did not like to think of Angie Kinyon alone with Nevers. The more he thought of it, the more he was sure she was not safe, that Nevers had wanted him away.

They worked their way back to their horses and both men mounted and headed away. Ortmann heard them going and swore softly. He hesitated, wanting to follow them, but he remembered Blaine's admonition. No matter what, he was to stay put.

"That way," Blaine had said grimly, "I won't be worried about who I shoot at. I know I won't have any friends out there!"

Ortmann fixed a meal and ate it at a table where he could watch the road. He sat that way until the sun faded and the night crawled down along the mountain sides.

Night came to the cabin in the sycamores. It gathered first in the stable, then in the yard under the trees. One by one the men slipped into the rear door of the house, ate and slipped back. Fox came and when he did, he checked the girl's bonds, freed her of the gag and made her coffee.

"You take it easy," he said, "an' you won't get hurt."

"Take it easy?" she asked bitterly. "While you kill a better man than all of you?"

The night drew on. A mocking bird spent most of it rehearsing in the sycamore nearest the house. Fox spent it lying on a horse blanket with a gun in his hand. Angie slept, awakened, then slept again.

On the bench among the cedars Utah Blaine was stretched out on his stomach. He had his blanket over him and he was comfortable despite the chill. He was exactly one thousand feet above the little ranch. From his vantage point he could see it plainly except for the places where the thick foliage of the sycamores prevented his getting a view of the yard and the back door.

Angie's mare was in the corral, and his dun was there. Yet he saw nothing of Angie. He had arrived just before night, and after it was dark he could see nothing but the lights and shadows cast by the moon and the mountains. There had been a light in the house, in the kitchen. It continued to be in the kitchen except once when it was carried into another room and then back. Several times he heard a door close.

All the arrivals had reached the ranch before he had a chance to see them. Nevertheless, Blaine knew they would be watching this place. He drew back from the edge and lighted a cigarette. It was growing colder yet he dared not build a fire. Still, he would wait. If she was down there alone, she was all right. If she was not, there would be some sound, some warning.

He would wait until morning. That would be soon enough to go.

Fox lifted his head suddenly. He heard footsteps within the house. He heard the boards creak softly. A door opened. He got to his feet and with a word to his men, moved swiftly.

Like a wraith he slipped into the house. By the shadow on the floor from the dimmed lamp he knew he was right. Nevers was standing over the horrified girl who could only stare at him. He was standing there, leering at her, his eyes wicked.

"This ain't your station, Russ."

Nevers' face twisted with fury. He turned sharply. "Damn you, Lee! Why don't you mind your own business?"

"This is my business." Fox was calm but his eyes had started their queer burning. "I don't want to get hung!"

"You go back where you belong!" Nevers said harshly.

"Not me," Fox grinned. "I'm stayin' here. You go to the stable."

"Like hell!" Nevers exploded.

Lee Fox tipped his rifle ever so slightly until the muzzle was pointing at Nevers' body. "Then shuck your gun, Russ. You go or one of us dies right here!"

Russ Nevers had never known such hatred as he now felt. He stared at Fox for a long instant. Then he wheeled. "Oh, hell! If you want to be a fool about it!"

He walked from the house and let the door slam behind him. Utah Blaine heard that door slam. It worried him.

CHAPTER XXI

IN THE DARKNESS Utah Blaine came down the steep side of the bench. Instinctively, he felt that he was headed for a showdown. When the first gray ap-

180

peared in the sky, he was standing in the brush not fifty yards from the corral, and no more than eighty yards from the cabin under the sycamores.

He took his time, lighting a cigarette and waiting, studying the house. There was no movement or sign of life for several minutes, and when it did come it was only a slow tendril of smoke lifting from the chimney. He studied it with furrowed brow, trying to recall if Angie had ever said anything about her hour of rising.

There was no wind and the sky was clear with promise of a very hot day. Utah was tired but ready. He could feel the alertness in his muscles, and that stillness and poise that always came to him in moments of great danger.

His wool shirt was stiff with sweat, dust, and dried blood. His body had the stale old feeling of being long without a bath. There was a stubble of coarse beard on his jaws, and as he stood there he could smell the stale sweat of his own body, the dryness of the parched leaves, the smell of fresh green leaves. He could hear the faint rustle of the river, not far off.

The slow tendril of smoke lifted lazily into the sky. Suddenly, the smoke grew blacker, and his eyes sharpened a little. He drew deep on the cigarette and watched. An oil-soaked cloth—something—suddenly the smoke broke sharply off. There was a puff, a break, another puff, another break!

Someone within the house—it could only be Angie —was signaling, warning him!

There was a sharp exclamation from the corral. A man Utah had not seen suddenly reared from behind the water trough and sprinted for the back door, cursing as he ran.

Utah Blaine smiled bleakly. "Good girl!" he said. "Oh, very good!"

Her ruse had been successful. He heard sharp talk, Angie's voice, then another man interposed. He listened, but could not make out the words. The voice sounded like that of Lee Fox.

The man came out the back door, glanced hurriedly around and went in a crouching run toward the water trough where he vanished from sight. The man was a rider for Fox. Blaine had seen him but once, but had heard the man called Machuk.

Thoughtfully, Utah surveyed the yard. There was a man in the corral. There was a man in the house and there would, without doubt, be one in the stable.

How many in all? Fox did not have as many hands as Nevers, but there could be six or seven men here. More likely there were four or five. And most serious of all, Rink Witter and Hoerner were unaccounted for. Utah finished his cigarette, dropped it and then carefully rubbed it out with his toe.

To hurry would be fatal. First he must find out for sure how many men were here, and unless he was mistaken he would soon have his chance. They had set a trap for him and were waiting, but that fire could only mean breakfast, coffee at least.

Utah grinned wryly, his green eyes lighting with a sort of ironic humor. He could do with some coffee himself. He studied the house speculatively, but the back door was covered by at least one man. Moreover, he could not move to the right because several magpies were scolding around and if he came closer would make enough fuss as to give him away.

There was a deadfall behind him and he sat down on the slanting trunk of the tree and waited.

He could hear the rattle of dishes within the house. Had it been Nevers in there he would have gone in. With Nevers there was a chance of bluffing him out of a shooting. If shooting there had to be, killing Nevers would not remain on his conscience. Lee Fox was another thing. There was no chance of bluffing any man on such a hair trigger as Fox. Moreover, Utah understood Fox's position and appreciated it.

He took out the makings and built another cigarette, taking his time. Impatience now would ruin everything. Now that he was here, now that he could see, the waiting would be harder on them than on him. They would break first.

A half-dozen plans occurred to him and were dismissed as foolhardy or lacking in the possibility of a decisive result. He saw Angie come to the door and throw out some water, saw her hesitate just a minute, and then call out to Machuk. The Table Mountain rider got up from behind the trough and went to the house. Utah heard dishes rattle, and the sound spurred his own ravenous hunger. After awhile, Machuk slipped out and returned to his place behind the trough, calling as he did so to another man. Utah could not distinguish the name.

This man walked with a peculiar droop to one shoulder. He passed the corral, coming from somewhere near the woodpile. That pegged three of them. Where were the others? One in the stable, certainly.

After awhile the man with the drooping shoulder came out of the house. He paused near the trough and Blaine heard his voice clearly. "Lee figures it won't be much longer."

"I hope not. I'm full up to here with settin' here in the dust."

"Gonna be a hot day, too."

"Yeah."

"Well, I gotta call Nevers." The man moved on and paused at the stable.

Nevers crossed the yard to the back door. He looked ugly. His face was black with a stubble of beard and Utah Blaine studied him shrewdly. Nevers was hopping. He was ready to go, just any time. He was a strange combination of qualities. At no time a good man, he had been on the side of decency by accident only. Now he was over the edge. He would not go back.

Nevers entered the house and there was the rattle of dishes again, and then Nevers' voice lifted. "Who's off station now?" he demanded.

Somebody, probably Fox, spoke in a lower tone. Then Nevers replied, "Oh, yeah? You'll butt in the wrong place, sometime, Lee! Damn you, I'll—"

The words trailed off with some kind of an interruption, and then Utah heard an oath from the house. "What is she anyway? Nothin' but a damned—"

"*Don't say it!*" That was Fox, definitely. The man's voice was sharp, dangerous. Utah tensed, ready to move forward. What was the matter with Nevers? Couldn't he see the man was on a hair trigger? For that matter, Nevers was, too. But not like Lee Fox. In a fight between the two, Fox was top man—any time.

Nevers must have realized it, for he could be heard growling a little. Finally, he came from the house and walked back to the stable, picking his teeth and muttering.

Utah waited . . . and waited. There were no more. Four was all. And he had them all spotted.

This could be the showdown. He knew where Nevers was. If Nevers was out of it he might reach some settlement with Fox. The Table Mountain rancher was rational enough at times. It was Nevers then. Nevers was the man to get.

Angie was safe enough with Lee Fox. His brow furrowed. Where was Ben Otten? In town? On the run?

Utah moved back into the brush, taking plenty of time. He worked his way around through the brush, avoiding the corral, and making for the back of the stable. He was tempted to move up on the man behind the woodpile, but did not. Avoiding him, he finally reached the stable. Here he had to leave the brush and move out into the open. Moving carefully, he made it to the corner. Then he stepped past the corner to merge with the shadow of a giant tree. One more step and he could get inside the stable with Nevers.

The stable was of the lean-to variety: the front closed across two-thirds of its face, with doors open at each side. It was through one of these doors that Utah expected to step. He knew Nevers was watching from the other door. He could see occasional movement there.

Utah hesitated, then stepped out. Yet even as he stepped he heard a cold, triumphant voice behind him.

"Been watchin' for you, Blaine!"

Utah turned, knowing what he would see. Rink Witter was standing there, not thirty yards away. He had come from the rocks near the trail from the river. Twenty yards further to the right was Hoerner.

Utah Blaine was cold and still. He was boxed: Nevers behind him, Witter and Hoerner in front; Fox at the house, and his two hands.

Six of them. "This is it, Utah," he whispered to himself. "You've played out your hand."

Yet even as he thought this, his mind was working. There was no chance for him to come out of this alive. The thing to do was take the right ones with him. Rink, definitely. Rink and Nevers. That meant a quick shot at Rink—but not too quick. Then a turn and a shot that would nail Nevers.

After that, if he was still alive, he could get into the stable. But all this meant ignoring the fire of four men, one of them a killer for hire—Hoerner— a man skilled in his business.

Utah Blaine stood beside the tree, his feet apart, his head lowered just a little, and he looked across the hot bare ground of morning at the blazing blue- white eyes of Rink Witter. All was very still. In the house a floor board creaked. Somewhere a magpie called. And Utah Blaine knew the girl he loved was in that house ... depending on him.

Then mounting within him he felt it, the old driv- ing, the surge of fury that came with the fight, the old berserk feeling of the warrior facing great odds. Suddenly doubt and fear and waiting were shed from him, and in that moment he was what he had been created for: a fighting man—a fighting man alone, facing great odds, and fighting for the things he valued.

He looked, and then suddenly he started to chuckle. It started deep down within him, a sort of ironic humor, that he, Utah Blaine, after all his care- ful figuring had been trapped, surrounded. He laughed, and the sound cracked the stillness like a bullet shattering thin glass.

"Glad to see you here, Rink," he said. "I was afraid you'd be late for the party!"

"I'm goin' to send you to hell, Blaine!" Rink's voice was low, cold.

Utah Blaine wanted to shatter that coldness. He wanted to break that dangerous icy calm. "You?" Utah put a sneer in his voice. "Why, Rink, without help you never saw the day you could send me anywhere! I've seen you draw, Rink. You're a washwoman, so beggarly slow I'd be ashamed to acknowledge you a Western man. You—a gunfighter?"

He laughed again. "As for sendin' me to hell, with all this help you might do it. But you know what, Rink? If I go to hell I'll slide through the door on the blood I drain from you an' Nevers. I'll take you two sidewinders right along, I'll—" He had been talking to get them off edge, and now— "take *you!*"

Incredibly fast, his hands flashed for their guns. Rink was ready, but the talk had thrown him off. Yet even without that split second of hesitation he could never have beaten that blurring swift movement of hands, the guns that sprang up. His own gun muzzle was only rising when he saw those twin guns and knew that he was dead.

He knew it with an instant of awful recognition. It seemed that in that instant as if the distance was bridged and he was looking right into the blazing green eyes of Blaine. Then he saw the flame blossom at the gun muzzle and he felt the bullet hit him, felt himself stagger. But he kept on drawing. And then the second bullet, a flicker of an instant behind the first, hit him in the hip and he started to fall.

His gun came out and he fired and the bullet hit the tree with a thud. With an awful despairing he realized he was not going to get even one bullet into Blaine, and then he screamed. He screamed and lunged up and fired again and again, his bullets going wild as death drew a veil over his sight and pulled him down ... down ... down.

Blaine had turned. Those two shots had rapped out as one and he spun, getting partial shelter from the tree, and in the instant of turning he saw an incredible thing: instead of firing at him, Nevers lifted his gun and shot Lee Fox in the stomach!

Fox stared at him, his eyes enormously wide, the whites showing as he staggered down the steps, trying to get his gun up. "I should—I should have—killed you!" His head turned slowly, with a sort of ponderous dignity and he looked at Blaine. "Kill him," he said distinctly. "He is too vile to live!" And Lee Fox fell, hitting the ground and rolling over.

Hoerner was running and now he was behind Blaine. He fired rapidly into Utah's back. He shot once ... twice ... three times.

The yard broke into a thunder of shooting and Blaine, shot through and through, staggered out from the tree. He slammed a shot into Nevers that ripped the rancher's shoulder; a second shot that knocked the gun from his hand. Turning, Blaine dropped to one knee, red haze in his eyes, and smashed out shots at Hoerner.

He saw the big body jerk, and he shifted guns and shot again and saw Hoerner falling. Then Utah turned back and he saw Nevers standing there, his right side red with his own blood.

"You're a murderer, Nevers!" Blaine's voice was utterly cold. "You started this! You were there with Fuller when they hung Neal! I heard your voice! You were behind it! Good men have died for you!"

Utah Blaine's gun came up and Nevers screamed.

Then Blaine shot him through the heart, and Nevers stood there for an instant, rocking with the shock of another bullet and then fell against the tree. The man with the drooping shoulder was lifting a Winchester and taking a careful sight along it when a rifle roared from the house door.

Amazed, Utah turned his head. Angie stood in the doorway, her father's Spencer in her hands. Coolly, she fired again, and Blaine looked toward the corral. "Come out, Machuk! Come out with your hands up!"

There was a choking cry, then Machuk's voice, "Can't. You—you busted my leg!"

Blaine turned and stared at Angie. One hand clung to a tree trunk. His body sagged. "Angie—you—you—all right?"

Then he heard a thunder of hoofs and he fell, and the ground hit him and he could smell the good fresh dust of the cool shadows. He heard the crinkle of a dried leaf folding under his cheek and the soft . . . soft . . . softness of the deep darkness into which he was falling away.

He opened his eyes into soft darkness. There was a halo of light nearby. The halo was around a dimmed lamp, and it shone softly on the face of the girl in the chair beside his bed. She was sleeping, her face at peace. At his movement, her eyes opened. She put out a quick hand. "Oh, you mustn't! Lie still!"

He sagged back on the pillow. "What—what happened?"

"You were wounded. Three shots. You've lost a lot of blood."

"Nevers? Rink?"

"Both dead. Rals Forbes was here, and Padjen

stayed here. He's sleeping in the other room. Rocky White was here, too."

"White?"

"He's the new marshal of Red Creek."

White, a tall rugged young puncher, looked like a good man. So much the better.

"What happened to Ben Otten?"

"Nevers killed him the night before you got here. Ben came here—for what I don't know—and Nevers shot him. Maybe he thought he was you. Maybe he didn't care. His body was lying in the stable all night and all the morning before the fight."

Otten . . . Nevers . . . Witter. And then Miller and Lud Fuller, and before them Gid Blake and Joe Neal . . . and for what?

"Country's growin', Angie," he whispered, "growin' up. Maybe this was the last big fight. Maybe the only way men can end violence is by violence, but I think there are better ways."

"They are setting up a city government in Red Creek," Angie said. "All of them are together."

"That's the way. Government. We all need it, Angie." He was silent. "Government with justice . . . sometimes the words sound so . . . so damn' stuffy, but it's what men have to live by if they will live in peace."

"You'd better rest."

"I will." He lay quiet, staring up into the darkness. "You know," he said then, "that 46—it's a good place. I'd like to see the cattle growin' fat on that thick grass, see the clear water flowin' in the ditches, see the light and shadow of the sun through the trees. I'd like that, Angie."

"It's yours. Joe Neal would like it too. You held it for him, Utah."

"For him . . . and for you. Without you it wouldn't be much, Angie."

She looked over at him and smiled a little. "And why should it be without me?" she asked gently. "I've always loved the place . . . and you."

He eased himself in the bed and the stiffness in his side gave him a twinge. "Then I think I'll go to sleep, Angie. Wake me early . . . I want to drink gallons and gallons of coffee . . ." His voice trailed away and he slept, and the light shone on the face of the woman beside him. And somewhere out in the darkness a lone wolf called to the moon.